THE TOADSTONE

A MURDER MYSTERY

Anne Gumley

Order this book online at www.trafford.com
or email orders@trafford.com

Most Trafford titles are also available at major online book retailers.

Printed in the United States of America.

ISBN: 978-1-4669-6463-1 (sc)
ISBN: 978-1-4669-6464-8 (hc)
ISBN: 978-1-4669-6465-5 (e)

Library of Congress Control Number: 2012919718

Trafford rev. 11/07/2012

Trafford
PUBLISHING·   www.trafford.com

North America & international
toll-free: 1 888 232 4444 (USA & Canada)
phone: 250 383 6864 ♦ fax: 812 355 4082

Contents

By the same author

To my three sons,
Julian, Nigel, Andrew.

Sweet are the woes of adversity which, like the toad, ugly and venomous, wears yet a precious jewel in its head.

"As You Like It"
Shakespeare

Prologue—1646

Market day in the city of Chester was always busy and noisy with the cries of vendors offering a variety of cut price goods and buyers looking for a bargain. Pickpockets mingled freely, often leaving satisfied with their day's work,

The air was bitterly cold. Even parts of the River Dee were frozen, the winter of 1646 one of the coldest on record. Normally the cold temperatures would have kept many at home preferring to huddle around their fires, but today was different, curiosity mingled with a primitive fear poured out adrenaline that overcame everything else.

The road that weaved through the city towards the gallows about a mile away was lined with young and old alike, all keen to catch a glance of the witch that would end her journey there on the stake.

The expectation of catching a glimpse of the famous Witch-Finder General astride his black horse moved the crowd forward like a long snake, only to be forced back by the Mounted Marshals that rode ahead clearing the road for the procession. Cursing and pushing heightened by the excitement; mingling with an unaligned fear that suddenly eased to silence as the Witch-Finder approached.

Most of those braving the cold had ventured out to see Beth Simkins who had murdered her husband by witchcraft. Rumours abounded of her dreadful deed and her meddling in the dark powers, even to having a three-legged cat as a familiar who spat when looked at. Gossip travelled fast; beginning in one tavern and subsequently embellished in each telling in the alehouses.

Some said she was from Northwich; others Macclesfield or Alderly and still others even went as far as saying she was from the dark peaks of Derbyshire.

Nearer the truth was that she was from the small market town of Danesbury. Interrogated by the Witchfinder and, after a short trial and sentencing at the Cheshire Assizes, was sent to languish in the city jail for more than three weeks from where her deeds were talked of in whispers.

Gossip abounded that her nurse too had been accused of witchcraft but had vanished into thin air along with Beth's son. Twice the nurse had been seen riding a huge black boar, the child clinging to her waist as the moon waned.

The neighbouring landowners, the Ravenscrofts gave evidence to the fact that they believed their harvest had been bewitched and had caused the local streams to dry up, their cattle dying and all manner of misfortunes had happened since Ralph Simkins had taken a wife. The Simkins land itself however had always prospered greatly, the river always swollen even after periods of low rainfall.

When the maid found Ralph Simkins dead in his bed of no known ailment, rumours became more exaggerated and the Witch-Finder General was sent for.

The Assizes had been crowded with the curious and variant stories were told of the trial. Pin-prickers had claimed she showed lack of sensitivity. Although it was also said she was only half conscious with jail fever during her trial.

A maid had testified that her mistress and her old nurse had made brews and hearing strange chanting behind locked doors. A bird in a cage in the kitchen was found dead one morning, when only the day before it was singing merrily.

A low murmur was heard from the galleries of the court as the maid spoke of a toadstone ring her mistress valued that had since disappeared. After a short review of the facts of the case a sentence was passed by the court and, as compensation for past losses, the land farmed by the Simkins line was to revert to their neighbours, the Ravenscroft family, while all remaining monitory goods were to go to the Crown for the payment of officials.

Based on all the evidence presented to the court, the verdict was passed. Beth Simkins was to be burnt at the stake.

Fed by the energy of their fellow spectators, the inborn fear of witchcraft was pushed aside, so eager was the desire to look on the said witch. Even so, there were still many in the crowd with fingers crossed, crucifixes held and lucky charms palmed, just in case the eyes of the accused rested on them as she passed by. When their turn came to sneak a glimpse at the passing cart, their own image of Beth Simkins was disappointing. Her small and thin appearance made her look more like a child. Half lying in the straw, head bowed and knees blackened with dirt and tucked up beneath her: both feet and hands tied with a coarse rope that showed signs of blood. Long hair, once fair, dangled over her face hiding it. She looked a pitiful sight. Occasionally someone would sigh and leave the crowd, deep in thoughts edged with pity.

Although all eyes sought the figure in the cart, they were lowered or looked away from the face of the Witch-Finder whose own piercing gaze seemed to search the crowd like some bloodhound on a scent trail.

Someone had thrown a sack around her shoulders, but still Beth shivered. Not only had her body seemed frozen but also her mind. She tried to think clearly but it all now appeared so disjointed. Loud voices: her limbs being pulled and prodded, questions, shouting, the cold, so very cold. She recalled the dampness of the stone hole of the gaol; the wreaking smells of urine and rotting rat carcases, pinpricks burning like fire. The image of fire brought the present moment back to her.

'Oh dear Lord, please help me bear all this.' Her parched lips moved but the words remained inside

The cart suddenly rocked dangerously as her dirty fingers poked through the wooden slats. The tight rope dug harshly into her wrists pulling at the tender skin. Now every movement of the cartwheels increased the pain.

The bodily pain brought back the present moment thrusting the sensation deep into her heart. A vivid picture of her son arose and again her lips moved beseeching God to give help to Martha and to her only offspring, now in Martha's care. Nothing now mattered; her old nurse and her son should be far away from all this and safe.

On route the crowd became thicker, the blurred images of the people passing by in a sort of haze of distorted faces. Soon the cart would pass the gallows and then____. She didn't want to think about it, her mind becoming cloudy again and the cold raw weather enfolded her into its own cocoon. Now there was only the rhythmic rattle of the wheels and the swish of the horse's tail in front.

The bumps on the road became more pronounced but the rawness of her wrists and ankles faded as she slipped in and out of the silent terror that held her prisoner. She tried to remember what her gaoler had told her.

"The executioner will tie a rope around thy neck, and thou wilt die of strangulation not the burning."

It seemed of little comfort at the time, but now a blessing as the present again returned. The crowd already assembled were silent this time, standing and watching in some sort of anticipation.

Raising her head as the cart stopped, she saw what she dreaded. The stake already piled with tar barrels and bundles of faggots. It stood alone, awaiting its victim, the small ladder placed beside a platform atop the wood.

'Oh God,' she prayed again. 'Not this, please not this.' Where was the rope that was promised? With panic in her eyes, she searched around the thick stake 'til she saw it resting on a peg off to one side.

Bile pumped up from her stomach, seeping down the sides of her mouth, releasing an acid flavour. Her legs gave way, no longer able to hold up her slender frame, as the liveried attendants cut the bonds and brought her to her feet. She felt her body being half lifted, half dragged from the cart leaving sharp wooden splinters piercing the flesh. She tried to cry out but the chanting of the crowd now drowned her voice.

'Burn the witch_____, burn the witch.'

It grew to a crescendo, blocking out the loud thumping of her racing heartbeats. A sea of blurred heads swam before her. The tightness was increasing around her chest. Even within her panic state, she knew it was only the solid stake behind her and the rope that held her upright. For one brief moment she wondered what she was standing on for the surface felt sticky and cold. She wanted to move her shoulders, the pain stabbing like a knife through the sockets.

'The smell, what was it?' It wasn't her own feces or urine that now ran down her legs. No, it was another smell, one from her childhood.

'Tar.' She recalled the cook had explained how tar was used to help chest ailments. She wanted to stay in the past, the comfortable house the daily routine, it helped block out all the horror, but the pain and fear brought the present moment back with a vengeance. Sobs welled up that stuck in her dry throat, choking and tightening her muscles.

'Water!' . . . visions of clear cool water floated across her mind, bringing the agony to a desperate pitch. Another smell, this time she was quick to recognize it, for it brought stinging smoke that blurred her vision.

Wood crackled its sound mingling with the roar of the crowd. A layer of smoke drifted upwards. The tight ropes binding her chest gave no room for the muscles to expand. Coughing came in short bursts, bulging the veins in the throat to bursting point. A soot-speckled rivulet of tears ran unabashed from stinging eyes. Then as the smoke cleared, a terrible searing pain shot up her legs. Her cry of anguish was drowned by the roar from the spectators. Then just as suddenly as it started, there descended a great silence as the flames leapt up from within the drying woodpile. Some crossed themselves; others touched their toadstones or amulets. A few shook their heads and lowered their eyes, remembering her generosity when the harvest was bad. An aged woman was pushed forward, her once quality clothes now torn and stained. The shawl wrapped around her covered a baby, its small head held against her breast as if to protect it from the vision before them. Gingerly the crowd parted, heads hanging low and shamefaced; the fever pitch of hysteria calming with the brutality of reality.

Then as if some energy had been picked up from this source, the condemned woman's head lifted and through the haze, her eyes picked out the group standing to one side.

Her gaze fell on a figure standing by the Witch Finder. She heard a small sharp laugh emerge from her scorched lips before choking on the acid smoke as she inhaled. Ravenscroft her accuser stood there too, a satisfied smirk on his face. The executioner held his burnt hand close to his body, caused unexpectedly by the flames that had made him drop the rope. He knew he would never forget the terrible screaming that followed his failure of duty would produce. With one last effort to revenge herself in the only way able, she summed up the last of her dying energy and to the horror of the crowd, her voice rang out loud and true.

'I damn you Ravenscroft: You and all your descendants.'

Then as if by a preordained signal, the tar bucket under her feet caught alight and a flaming inferno burst forth, accompanied by such screaming that it continued to haunt many a soul present on that day for the rest of their lives.

Against the breast of a shawl covered and trembling spectator, a baby let out a wailing cry.

Chapter 1

The monotonous rhythm of the train wheels and the flickering images of scenery caused Ernest to quietly slip into a half hypnotic trance. Pictures arose vividly from his subconscious, vast areas covered with tall pine trees, large lakes stretching out to the horizon that resembled seas. White capped mountains and straight roads that went on forever. Concrete jungles of tall buildings that shadowed busy streets, and Rita's happy face explaining Canada to him.

The man sitting opposite from him in the train coughed and changed the position of his crossed legs.

The trance broken, Ernest raised his head, the images dissolving. He felt the knot in his stomach tighten again, the stress of the last few days returning.

The same question kept popping up.

'Had he done the right thing in returning to England without her?' Rita had thought so, she being the first to suggest it.

'Lisa will need you,' she had added being as practical as ever. 'I will sell the apartment and be back with you in no time.' Still it didn't seem right, him having to shorten his honeymoon. Ernest felt torn between two poles.

Leaning back and turning his head, he gazed out of the window. The busy airports, London Underground and Euston Station seemed a long way away: the open countryside bringing a sense of homecoming. Canada was majestic, but England was lovely. Ernest played with the two words for a while before deciding no one could call Canada lovely. Grand, yes; marvellous, even spectacular, but lovely only belonged to the English countryside. Musing on the thought, he suddenly became aware of his companion who was clearing his throat. They looked at each other and smiled as strangers do, not too inviting but more as an acknowledgement of each other's presence.

'Crewe?' Ernest's question sounded blunt but it opened a line of communication.

'Yes'

'Me too,' replied Ernest.

Silence followed, which only served the purpose of heightening their awareness and for quiet study of each other. The man opposite Ernest seeing someone his own age, sixty or so, slightly overweight around the girth, judged to be tall by the length of his legs and size of his footwear. Thinning, salt-and-pepper-coloured hair, pleasant face but heavy brows with brooding eyes. Clothes that suggested a holiday abroad, a sweatshirt covering a plaid shirt, white socks and sandals all too new to be his normal attire.

Ernest's assessment was quicker and less focused on the outward appearance. A quick scan of the man's features provided much about his character. Thin brows brought together by a deep furrow, his eyes suggesting an avid reader or worrier. Sunken cheeks tinged slightly yellow gave a clue to poor health. Likewise yellowing; poorly kept teeth indicated a lack of care. Ernest had eliminated lack of money by the quality of the material of his sports jacket. Though well used; indicated by the scuffmarks on the leather elbow patches.

'Been abroad?' the man asked.

Ernest suddenly became conscious of his floppy Canadian holiday clothes and found himself explaining his trip to Canada, his late in life marriage to his childhood sweetheart during her extended visit to the UK from the Colonies.

'We went back to Canada for a holiday and to sell her apartment there before returning. However a friend's mother died and we decided I should come back earlier to help out.'

'Good friends are hard to come by. So many young ones are only out for themselves these days,' his travelling companion added with a sigh.

'And you?' Ernest asked with interest. He was now ready for conversation as it stopped his negative thinking. He sat straighter in his seat.

'Doing a little research on families.' The answer was not very informative, but such research was very popular nowadays as census information was available over the Internet. Ernest nodded and leaned forward holding out his hand.

'Ernest Heath, retired police inspector,' his eyes twinkled for a moment as he noted the man's look of surprise.

Clasping Ernest's hand in a surprisingly strong grip, his companion introduced himself.

'Thomas Reece, retired professor of medieval history at Oxford.'

Bang on, Ernest congratulated himself silently, he had already decided he was some sort of a bookworm. His eyes travelled to the man's hand holding his.

'Unusual ring you have there,' he said, his eyes lingering on a rather large ornate silver ring with some sort of stone set in its centre. His first guess was it was Celtic, as the Celtic designs were becoming popular these days, but it looked too worn and old to have been made recently.

'What's the stone?' He leaned forward to take a closer look as the wearer's hand which was flattened out on his knee and the fingers stretched wide so the ring could be displayed.

'It's called a toadstone.' The professor looked up from the object smiling as he scoured Ernest's quizzical face.

'A what?' The question came as no surprise to the owner as he had heard the same response many times before. The unusual ring was pulled off and handed over.

Ernest held it up to the light from the window. The stone was the size of his fingernail; its colour was pale brown with a bluish spot in the middle that looked like an eye. It also had a tiny bright line on the upper left hand side.

'They were very popular around the 1600's and used for a variety of things, including detecting poison by changing colour.' The professor glanced at Ernest's uncommitted expression before adding, 'and protecting the cow's milk from being cursed by witches.'

'Good grief,' uttered Ernest.

The professor sat back and eyed his companion for a moment before saying,

'Are you superstitious about anything?'

'Walking under ladders' was the quick reply, 'although I guess I am edging my bets about something falling on me.' He thought for a moment about the question. 'I don't really know why I throw salt over my shoulder or knock on wood but I do.'

'What about your parents?'

'Cannot say, mum died young, the only superstition my dad had was using the strap regularly in case he lost the use of his arm muscles.'

The professor gave him a sympathetic look.

'Bad was it?'

Ernest nodded, and then continued answering the first question. 'My grandmother wouldn't have lilac or hawthorn blossom in the house.'

The professor crossed his legs and sat back, his position indicating he was at ease talking to a stranger.

'I reckon not much has changed then.'

Ernest grinned at the smooth way the man had taught him something of his past and present culture.

The professor looked down at his ring.

'These toadstones were much sort after to wear as amulets against witchcraft and bad luck.'

'Well I never.' Ernest was suddenly caught up in a subject he knew little about. What a tale to tell Rita and Lisa, then surprised himself by asking, 'you said you were a professor of medieval history, aren't the sixteen hundred's rather late for your line of research? I thought medieval belonged to the thirteenth and fourteenth centuries.'

'You are quite right,' his companion confessed. 'But my real passion has always been related to researching witch hunters in England during the reign of James the First.'

This man's hobby is unreal, mused Ernest to himself while studying his companion's facial flush and bright eyes. Even though he mocked, there was a little place deep down within Ernest that envied the passion now carried into retirement.

The voice continued, 'you and I are something alike. You like to solve crimes of today, whilst I go back so much further in time. But I'm sure you understand that feeling whenever a case is at the point of being solved.'

Ernest, acknowledged the point being made and nodded, even if it was on very different timescales and investigative methods. Justice was the same.

He felt himself being studied again, as if the informant was trying to find a better way of explaining himself.

'I'm not interested in black magic and sorcerers. No, my interest lies in the persecution of innocent people. Tried and condemned for no other reason than they maybe delivered someone's child who died. They were the scapegoats for other's fears or, more often than not, just plain greed. Condemn someone and if they're found guilty some their goods were sometimes given to the accusers.'

'Blimey.' Ernest could think of many a modern case that would equal that also. He settled back to hear more.

'Witch hunting came to its zenith with King James 1 when the king repealed the last witchcraft condemnation and replaced it with a far more severe one.'

A bulb switched on in Ernest's brain.

'King James was a protestant wasn't he?' Ernest's primary church schooling was still imparting its influence on him. The professor looked blank, but nodded, eager to keep the conversation going as not many people were interested in what he had to say since he retired.

'Yes indeed he was, but the burning of the so-called witches had already started in Europe. Unfortunately for the poor masses, the imagination of the writers became reality for those that read, namely the rich. The poor and illiterate were as always the targets and it was the women among them who were generally earmarked as potential victims.'

'Why women?' Ernest butted in, feeling Lisa's pleasure in this defence of her gender.

The professor looked undisturbed by the question. It was raised many times by his female students who really understood, but were often just making a point.

'Women had the power of life and death. They were the midwives and herbalists.'

'Makes sense,' admitted Ernest, while reminding himself again to just listen and not comment. His recall of historical events was never that good and he now felt a need to surprise Rita with this newfound information.

'A Witchfinder General was appointed by James I,' the voice carried on, 'and together with his assistants, they scoured the countryside for evidence of witchcraft. Many innocent people were thrown into prison and tortured; many dying of starvation or jail fever. Others strangled, hung or burnt.'

Ernest focused; 'Did the professor emphasize those burnt?' It was just a tiny thought that Ernest recognized and let go. It was all very real the way the professor told it, but there was one more question niggling him that he had to ask. 'You mentioned earlier you were getting off at Crewe Station. Are you doing research in that area or are you just visiting?'

The professor was looking at his watch. He leaned forward and gazed out of the train window, before adding;

'We're nearly there, another ten minutes or so.' He stood up, back towards Ernest and lifted a large black leather bag down. The question went unanswered.

They parted company as soon as the carriage door opened. Ernest made his way along the platform to the ticket gate, refusing a trolley from the porter and lengthening his steps to avoid being hassled by the taxis cruising around the entrance. He caught a glimpse of the professor getting into one, and then hurried over the road to the bus stop.

Ten minutes later he was watching the countryside pass again; the dull ache of depression descending again as he visualised a cold empty cottage and an empty bed awaiting him. Here he was alone again and Rita further away than ever. Then there was Lisa. What state would she be in? Did she really need him? The last time he saw her she was getting on just fine with that farmer friend of hers.

'Women seemed to be ruling my life these days,' he mused as he rolled his head around his shoulders. Christ it was good to be in his own country again. All that heat had got him down and those bloody mosquitoes saw him as fair game. The English blood is thin and they like new blood, a comment he'd often heard from Canadians which he tended to believe seeing how many times he was bitten.

'Well they can keep the darned things over there, and I'll keep my thin blood,' he mused. Once the silent conversation with himself was over, his thoughts turned to a nice cup of tea in his own armchair. Then, as the hunger began to remind he hadn't eaten much, he decided to visit Lisa first.

Chapter 2

Detective Sergeant Lisa Pharies glanced at the clock which displayed birds instead of numbers on the kitchen wall. She had done the same thing for the umpteenth time that morning. The large black finger clicked, and then moved to the red-breasted robin that denoted the top of the hour. It was two o'clock.

The image of Ernest's large comfortable frame stepping off the train at Crewe station brought a momentary relief from the anxiety that had plagued Lisa since finding her mother dead following a stroke a few days ago. It was shortly after her mother's death that she realized just how much she had valued her relationship with her former police colleague. The years she had worked with the now retired detective inspector as his detective sergeant had been the most satisfying period of her life. It had been herself that had cajoled him into buying a vacant cottage a few doors away from her own in the quiet village of Gelsby, and he had helped her through a difficult year following a series of homicides in the village.

Ernest, now happily married to his childhood sweetheart Rita, had become the family Lisa had been lacking. Ernest was very much the father figure to her, and Rita, with her practical nursing experience, had made life so much more tolerable by looking after her invalid mother and providing a shoulder to cry on over her own shattered and unfulfilled romances. Now two days before her mother's funeral she needed him more than ever.

Lisa glimpsed at the clock again and felt a twinge of guilt as she allowed thoughts of her own romances to be brought to the surface of her consciousness. Half in love with a man of the cloth, she'd found out he was her own cousin and it still disturbed her, even though she had told herself they had only been friends and had never let it go any further. Now she had Ted in her life, a good solid man who made it plain he was there to take care of her. The trouble was Lisa didn't want anyone to take care of her at thirty odd. She was much too independent or so she thought, until her mum died. Now she didn't want to be alone to brood, but needed someone around to voice her grief to and take care of the things that were piling up, but somehow Ted didn't fit the picture at all.

The kettle hissed as steam and water spitted from its spout. Lisa got up wearily and opened the cupboard door searching for a carton of teabags. After a while she found them hidden behind two new packets of loose tea.

There was something deliberate in the way Lisa pulled out a teabag on its string and whirled it around in the steaming water in her mug. Taking the mug back to the table, she lifted the teabag out and flung it into the sink with a well-practised aim.

She sighed, knowing that before Ted arrived she would take the discarded teabag and hide it under the kitchen rubbish. She just didn't need another lecture on the quality of the tea usually found in teabags.

Pulling her chair across the tiled floor, Lisa sat facing her computer where Ted had moved it into a small corner of the room. She muttered something under her breath about why he always insisted she turn the computer off after each session.

Turning the computer on deliberately, she pushed the long pad away that he'd brought for her to rest her wrists on while typing. Annoyance swept through her again. Why does he keep changing things? She didn't need yet another upgrade, just her old computer set up the way she had always had it and knew inside out.

'It's my bloody computer.' The words spilled out aloud filled with frustration as she noted he'd deleted her junk mail once again.

She would have readily admitted it was of no importance, but it was nevertheless her junk mail not his.

She answered a couple of e-mails from well wishing members of her unit sending her sympathy and telling her to make the most of her rest, but it didn't help to cheer her up as it made her feel that life went on very well without her at the police headquarters. She did however read the one from D.C. Smith, a new detective constable who had been assigned to her. He explained the new set-up following the replacement of Chief Inspector Edgeworth.

"Owen James is his name, from North Wales", the message read. Lisa smiled. With a name like that she didn't expect him to come from Manchester. She wrote back that cockie-leaky soup and welsh rarebit would probably now feature on the canteen menu, then deleted it as she decided D.C. Smith's mother would probably have never made it, or even knew what cockie-leaky or welsh rarebit was.

Jiten Smith's mother was Indian and Jiten had inherited his mother's bronze skin and jet-black hair. Everything about him shouted Indian apart from his very blue eyes and name, which was as English as fish and chips. Lisa hadn't had time to really get to know the new detective but liked his company and thought they'd make a good team.

She switched off the computer and wandered into the small lounge, sitting down in her usual seat opposite the armchair her mother had died in. Lisa gazed at the empty space with her mother's shawl draped over the back. It didn't take much to bring up the disfigured face of the former stoke victim and the pale grey piercing eyes filled with love.

Tears came unashamed and were followed by loud gulps of grief seeking to explode. Then stillness swept over her as she remembered that her mother had never been alone. She had always had a caring devoted daughter.

Lisa sat back closing her eyes and wondering what the future had in store for herself. She couldn't see herself as a farmer's wife and that's what she'd be if she married Ted, although in truth the subject had never come up. She loved her job in the police force and had always seen it as a career for life. Now all at once she was becoming aware of her life after retirement. Alone, no children and probably still in the same cottage she was born in. It was a sobering thought.

Looking at the two alternatives, the second made her relax more than the first, although much was left to be desired; someone to curl up with in bed, someone to voice concerns and problems to, someone to cook for. The latter thought causing a slight panic.

Opening her eyes she gave a little groan. She needed to think of something for dinner. Ernest would be hungry and she'd no food in. How many for dinner? She counted three fingers, muttering 'Ernest, Ted and herself.'

'Would the frozen shepherd's pie be enough?' she asked herself.

Getting up too quickly and making herself slightly dizzy, she hurried into the kitchen. Pulling the shepherds pie out of the small freezer compartment of the fridge, she mentally divided it by three. Satisfied there would be enough if a few frozen peas were added, she lifted out a carton of chocolate ice cream. There was some left in the bottom and some caked around the sides of it. Lisa visualised a tin of peaches topped with a spoonful of ice cream. Satisfied she was in control; she switched on the kettle and fiddled behind the packets of loose tea looking again for one of her favourite teabags.

The front door bell rang; three short bursts followed by a pause, then a long drawn out ringing signifying impatience.

'Dam,' she uttered pushing the teabag into the pocket of her jeans. 'He's early.'

She flew into the hallway, stopping for a second to push back the limp hair that had fallen out of the band tying her ponytail, and opened the door. Ted stood there looking slightly annoyed.

'I need a key' he said, pushing his way past her and as he did she became aware of a faint smell of manure entering with him.

Lisa watched as he sat on the bottom stair pulling off large boots that had a slight cake of farmland embedded in one of the soles. She coughed a short dry cough that Ernest would have immediately recognised as the beginning of stress.

'About that key,' Ted was saying as he was making his way down the hallway.

Lisa gingerly picked up his boots and placed them by the front door. The smell always slightly nauseated her as it always seemed to linger, even after he'd gone and she'd sprayed with deodorant.

'Give me yours and I'll get one cut,' Ted was saying from the kitchen as the sound of the computer could be heard being turned on. A knot wound itself up into her shoulders and a feeling of acid rising slightly from her stomach made her take a deep breath and tell herself she was just overly sensitive because of her loss. Things had changed for her and Ted was only expecting a normal relationship.

'I'll see to it, after the funeral,' she answered although somehow her reply wasn't as enthusiastic as it should have been. Ted however didn't seem to notice as he was already reading her e-mails she'd received and even the ones she'd replied to.

'This Indian fellow seems a bit of a jerk.' Ted laughed but there was a touch of disapproval in his voice.

Her shoulders knotted again, a little bit tighter this time. 'What do you mean by that?' she asked.

'I've heard that Hindu's believe in hundreds of gods, that's what.'

Lisa's shoulders tightened some more but like always when she was really angry, her voice was low and precise.

'Actually it is one of the world's major religions and has had a profound influence on many other religions including your own.' she said calmly placing two cups on their saucers. Her words were now said with some emphasis, as she knew that whenever Ted got into history of any sort, she always had the upper hand. Not that she knew a lot, but he knew less; his only really great interest was farming. Feeling more self-esteem now and better in control, she replaced her cup and saucer with her mug out of the sink and put a teabag in it, its dangling string deliberately turned in Ted's direction so he would notice.

'I'm just going to the loo Ted. Be a love and make a pot of tea for yourself. There's some of your favourite loose tea in the cupboard, I'll just have a tea bag.'

She closed the toilet door behind her and just sat on the closed seat. She took a deep breath and the knot lessened; her chest restriction easing. No one was going to dominate her and certainly not a person who smelt like his cows. Ernest would be home soon and suddenly all her bottled-up emotions would feel as if help was at hand.

'Sod the key,' she thought; pulling the chain and listening to the water wash the sides of the unused toilet bowl.

The computer was turned off and Ted was stirring the pot of tea. He put down the spoon and handed her the mug with the teabag dangling in it; a look of disapproval on his face.

'I've been thinking Lisa.' he said with some genuine feeling. 'Your mum could never afford a grave stone for your dad, but how about one now with both their names on.'

He paused, letting the words sink in before placing a hand over hers

.'I know your mum had no insurance or savings, being a widow, so I'd like to have one made for you, at my expense of course.'

All at once Lisa's past thoughts crumbled as she visualised her mum's and dad's names engraved forever on their grave. She knew her mother secretly had felt a sorrow when she visited the churchyard and stopped by a mound of earth that didn't say anything about who lay there.

The arm moved further around her shoulder and pulled her to a warm chest. This time the odour smelt very masculine and comforting. When few more words were whispered in her ear suggesting they go to her bedroom together she didn't object; she didn't want to be alone.

Lisa was hastily pulling on a sweater and urging Ted to get up when the doorbell rang.

'Ernest,' she breathed frantically, leaping about and almost tripping down the stairs in her haste to get to the front door. She flung the door open, and then stood for a moment with an amazed expression on her face. The man facing her was Ernest all right; there was no question about that, but he looked different. It took a second or two to realise it was his clothes. She'd never seen him in anything but a collar and tie. Sometimes he would don a sweater instead of his sports jacket but always a neat collar and tie.

Here he was now sporting a brightly coloured plaid open necked shirt over which he wore an oversized grey sweatshirt with some logo printed across the chest. She stared at him as he awaited his expected greeting, but quite forgetting the very Canadian apparel he was wearing. At last she threw herself at him with a big hug, then stepping back a little uncertain about her over-familiarity. Ernest chuckled as he lifted up his travel baggage.

'Haven't been home as yet.' he said. His smile became serious as he added, 'Lisa I'm so sorry about Emily, are you alright?'

Lisa nodded and coughed, while at the same time trying to hold back the tears.

'Cuppa?' she asked.

'Grand, I could do with wetting my whistle.' He lifted his bag into the hall.

'Ted's here,' Lisa announced when a noise was heard from upstairs.

'Going well?' Ernest asked with a slightly silly grin on his face. Lisa shrugged her shoulders and was noncommittal as Ted came bounding down the stairs.

'Good time in the Canada then, Ernest?' Ted slapped him on the back and led him into the lounge: shouting back to Lisa,

'Let's have a coffee and sandwich love.'

Lisa found herself plugging in the coffeemaker. She'd almost forgotten how to use it as "Instant" was her preference, but Ted had made it very clear if you drink coffee, drink only the real stuff leached from freshly ground beans; not from some manufactured freeze dried concoction.

She could hear Ted's voice rising as he gave his description of a Canada he'd never visited. Ernest looked at her curiously as she brought in a tray but try she might she couldn't stop the blushing she felt creeping into her cheeks.

'Ernest can eat more than that.' said Ted eyeing the sandwiches and hinting she make more. He turned to Ernest. 'Steak tonight, right off the cow.' He laughed, leaning back awaiting the expected sounds of enthusiasm.

The flush on Lisa's face darkened, the thought of her nice shepherd's pie fading and Ted fussing over the barbeque he'd bought for her second hand. She tried to stop the cough that was irritating the back of her throat.

Ernest wasn't quite sure what was wrong but something was, and for that he would have bet his last cigarette that lay in his pocket awaiting a non-smoking area for his occasional lapse. He placed his bet on knowing Lisa wasn't into meals that needed too much attention and the look on her face confirmed it.

'Better still, let me take you two out for dinner at the Horseshoe, then no one has to cook and we can all talk.' interrupted Ernest. He stood up and gave a little yawn raising his arms above his head. 'I'm more tired than I thought, the jet lag is worse coming back than going, and I guess I need some shut-eye before dinner.'

Ted didn't go to the door with them. He sat staring at the plate of sandwiches not sure what had happened to his plans. Lisa came back smiling.

Chapter 3

Ernest turned his key in the lock of his own cottage while at the same time kicking at the base of the heavy door by force of habit. Feeling a sharp pain across the toes of his left foot, he pulled back in surprise and stared down at his open-faced sandals, cursing under his breath. His new Canadian sandals had caused him nothing but grief, remembering how he nearly fell up the elevator at Heathrow. At the time he bought them, he'd told Rita he was quite happy in his size twelve black Clarks he'd always worn in the force, but she had insisted things were different now that he'd retired.

The slight annoyance with Rita vanished as he lugged his bag into the hall. There was a slight smell of damp as if the English weather had taken over the empty cottage. He felt a sudden loneliness and would have given anything at that moment to hear her voice.

He stood bag in hand at the end of the hallway, undecided whether to enter the kitchen or the lounge. Deciding there was nothing to go into the kitchen for, as the fridge would be empty; he made for his favourite chair and flopped down wearily then bent forward and turned on the gas fire. Nothing happened. Sighing deeply, he eased himself up making for the kitchen to turn on the gas at the meter and the main electrical supplies at the fuse box, but not before noticing the post stacked up on the kitchen table as he passed it.

Lisa had obviously been around. He knew straight away by the way she'd placed the post; bills piled up neatlyby size in one pile, flyers in another, and one solitary letter with no senders address which Ernest guessed had already been held up to the light. An odd smile flicked across his face; he'd trained Lisa well he thought.

Gathering up all the papers and envelopes, he picked up a bottle of wine and a glass and made a beeline for his chair, this time sinking into it with a contented sigh.

It wasn't long before the bottle of wine was half empty, the post still largely unread and a recent newspaper half opened across his lap. Ernest slid back in his chair, as was his habit. Resting his head on his upturned hand, he stared at the ceiling. His mind skipped briefly over images of airports, train-stations, before stopping to focus on his travelling companion on the train to Crewe and their conversation on witchcraft and its punishment during the middle ages in England. 'Funny old chap,' mused Ernest, his inner vision recalling the ring the man wore and the conversation they had had.

Toadstones?, that was a new one on Ernest. The professor had not mentioned where the stones came from and he had not asked, which was unlike him. Probably somewhere like the Blue John mines in Derbyshire, but why call them toadstones; he had no idea.

Ernest stirred and the wine glass; still half full of red wine wobbled on the arm of his chair. He grabbed it before it tipped and placed it on the hearth. Never do for Rita to find red stains around his chair he thought. Shifting his position and replacing his arms behind his head, he resumed his mental tracking.

'Burnt at the stake__,' the words popped up from half forgotten history lessons. Ernest recalled the stories of Queen Mary Tudor, or Bloody Mary as she was named for the burning of heretics. It was a great chance to swear without a clip around the ear. Then there was Joan of Arc, wasn't she burnt at the stake? Guy Fawkes? Here he stopped, uncertain of the way Guy Fawkes really died, despite the bonfires on the 5th day of November.

'All religious fanatics,' Ernest reasoned having little time for organised religion of any sort, especially after the series of deaths in his own village perpetrated by fundamentalism and an unstable mind.

Just on the verge of letting his daydreaming dissolve, a mental vision from long past popped into his mind.

Three of them, all ten-year-old boys playing around the wooden stocks in the market place, came to mind. They had been sitting on the rails of the cattle pens, watching the farmers moving their cows and pigs. Then they climbed over the town's old stocks, each having a go at placing their thin wrists through the worn holes, shouting to be released with promises to never steal again. When suddenly a large dried cow paddy hit Ernest square in the face when it was his turn. Unfortunately the middle of the paddy was not so dry and the soft middle caught Ernest with his mouth wide open as he attempted to scream.

Gulping and trying not to be sick, Ernest bent over the stone water trough and rinsed out his mouth. The taste and smell still lingering as he came up for air. Charlie Batts along with Jimmy Oaks had long since disappeared before he'd regained his self-control.

An old farmer was leaning over one of the iron railed enclosures watching him. A cigarette hung limply out of the corner of his mouth; the brown nicotine stain turning his large moustache ginger.

'Them's got thee there lad,' the Danesburyian accent slipped out with a chuckle. 'The witch them burnt in the old days had more than a cow patch thrown before them burnt her.' He puffed on the daggling cigarette after each sentence.

The witch___. Ernest's thoughts were back in the present time. Did Danesbury have its own witch? Was the professor doing research on a witch from around here, be it hundreds of years ago? Rita would be interested in that, mused Ernest before slipping into a deep sleep and dreaming he was playing marbles with toadstones that suddenly came alive and hopped away.

Awaking three hours later with a slight headache and dry mouth, he suddenly remembered he'd never phoned the Horseshoe about booking a meal. Sighing he got up and phoned Lisa

'Is six o'clock too late Lisa?' He enquired with a feigned concern, and for a second he'd wondered if he had misread his old colleague. There was a pause followed by Lisa's upbeat voice.

'Great for me Ernest; can't wait any longer to eat but I'm afraid Ted won't be able to make it, bringing the cows in and milking you see.' Ernest clenched his fist and gave a quick punch into the air. Then with a voice that didn't match his feelings said quietly,

'So sorry Lisa, it was the best I could do.'

'I bet it was gov,' came back her voice. She hoped her addressing him as "gov." would half convey she knew he was no fool.

By six thirty the two of them had settled down in the snug at the Horseshoe to a homemade steak and kidney pie and mushy peas. The wine bottle was half empty and in the last half hour Lisa felt more relaxed than she had been for days.

They talked about Emily; partly with sadness but now and then with a hearty laugh as they remembered the good parts. Over apple pie and cream, Ernest couldn't contain himself any more. His face became serious.

'What's wrong Lisa? The relationship with Ted isn't what you'd hoped for, eh?' It was the placing of the large firm hand of his over hers that brought tears to her eyes.

'Everything is fine; honestly. It's just that he wants to do so much for me.'

'Don't you mean he wants to do everything the way he wants it Lisa.' Ernest stirred his coffee, more by reflex, as he didn't take milk or sugar.

Lisa rolled her shoulders forward, a tight knot forming.

'It's just his way.' She suddenly felt dishonest to Ted and ungrateful for all his arranging of her mother's funeral and affairs. Then there was the gravestone. 'I don't know what I'd have done without him being around,' she said weakly. 'It is always the same, when he isn't there I only see the good things about him.'

'OK love, I'm only looking out for you.' He gave her hand a squeeze and sat back. 'More coffee?'

She nodded and looked around for the waiter when suddenly a big grin crossed her face. She stood up nearly knocking over her chair.

'Smithy,' she called out, indicating with her hand a place at their table.

To Ernest's surprise, it was not the waiter that had caught Lisa's attention, but a tall slim dusky skinned fellow who was making for the bar. He stopped, gave a short wave and crossed the floor. Ernest pulled up a chair and waited for the introductions.

'Smithy,' said Lisa, eagerly pulling him towards the chair. 'This is my old gov., Detective Inspector Heath; remember I told you all about him.'

Her guest smiled showing a set of teeth Ernest would have given his right arm for, whether in the mouth or a dental, it didn't matter. As Ernest's iron grip folded over the darker hand, a cultured English voice said.

'Detective Constable Smith, sir.'

Ernest caught Lisa smiling and he wasn't beyond himself in recognising the respect being offered.

'So,' said Ernest after ordering a round of drinks. 'What's new on the menu?' No one doubted it was any interesting police investigation that Ernest was referring to and not the pub's good food. The new occupant of the table looked at Lisa for confirmation and she nodded. However nothing of interest was offered apart from the usual traffic violations and a couple of incidents of domestic violence.

'Is this your regular?' asked Ernest, after hearing the new detective constable lived in the nearby town. He eyed the newcomer with interest. Maybe his preference for this neighbouring village pub was not totally without motive, and there was a genuine softness of concern about the impending funeral of Lisa's mother in his voice when he spoke to Lisa. Later when somehow they got around to life after death he offered his own belief system which proved different from Christianity, but interesting no less.

'We believe that nothing dies, but is born again to continue the spiritual journey. It may help you to think of your loss that way.' With that said he left, leaving Lisa staring after him and Ernest staring at Lisa, 'til she added simply,

'He is talking of reincarnation; it is rather nice way of looking at things isn't it.'

'Come on lass.' Ernest put his arm around her and led her through the pub dining room. He couldn't help thinking about the change that had taken place following the brutal murder of the barmaid last year. New management had brought in a different cliental, some for the food and others for the curiosity. However the bar saloon retained the strength of the local villagers and neighbouring farmers and as they were leaving, many offers of sympathy were given to Lisa, whom they had known all their lives.

Returning home, Ted's car was parked outside Lisa's cottage and Lisa stiffened visibly and touched Ernest's arm.

'Rita can be a bit bossy sometimes too can't she,' she said.

He stopped and thought for a while before explaining his own relationship with Rita.

'Rita has known me since I was five; she knows all my strengths and weaknesses. She doesn't ever put me down, but pushes me to only be the best I am.' He glanced down the road, the evening was closing in and quiet had descended. 'There's a world of difference in allowing someone to grow, or a taking away of their self-esteem.'

Chapter 4

Approximately half way between the village of Gelsby and its neighbouring town Danesbury, a lane branched off to the right. It wandered steadily downhill to the river and the old mill that had long ago been built on the river's bank.

Either side of the dusty lane thick brambles and tall grasses grew in the hedgerows, a breeding ground for small rodents that occasionally got hit by vehicles and on hot sunny days lay like flattened pieces of dried leather.

On the left hand corner of the lane's entrance stood a large Victorian gabled house. Its huge front bay windows overlooking the busy road, whilst the back of the house looked over the tree tops of the sprawling wood whose tree roots were firmly anchored into the steep hill. Beyond, marshes and green fields patterned the landscape before reaching the river.

Opposite the house and even grander in stature were two massive water towers that stood like fortresses. The five barred gate that gave entrance to a narrow pathway that reached them, lay broken and open; brambles and nettles having long taken root and had grown in between the spars. The older generations remembered the magic of imagination when the buildings turned into castles and a knight-errant could rescue damsels in distress. Sadly however the children of this generation didn't come any more, the TV and video games now fired their enthusiasm. The first of the disused water towers was built in 1874, after the town's existing water supply was judged the cause of typhoid outbreak; much later new ones had since taken their place the other side of the town.

The lane, always known as Mill Lane, had no destination apart from the mill and river. Once a silk mill, the huge water wheel turned continuously, driven by the flowing river's energy. Later with the arrival of electricity in the town, the old wheel race fell into disuse as the new technologies were quickly exploited and other manufacturing capabilities of the old mill developed.

A hundred years ago when industry began bringing families from the countryside in search of a better life, a row of cottages had been built at the side of the mill for the workers. Now the small two roomed cottages with the outside privies were derelict and overgrown, their grey stone crumbling and windows boarded up. The last one of the row however had survived and was still occupied.

The large house that sat at the lane's entrance and the land down to the river was owned by the Ravencroft family and had been handed down in a direct line from father to son. For four hundred years the Ravenscrofts had filled their pockets and bank balances from the proceeds of this land; the large red brick gabled house at the top of the hill giving credence to their wealth.

Another family, the Simkins; their ancestry just as old, had made their living as near as possible to a parcel of land, either working it or in the latter years by working at the mill. Now only two of the Simkins line remained, Jenny and her eight-year-old son Peter. There was no husband and the father of the young boy; a mystery. Jenny still occupied the cottage after her mother died.

Today Jenny had risen early. Leaving the cottage she pushed open the black iron gate that ended the lane and gave entrance to a field. She had always liked to walk amid the dew soaked grass with the scent of bluebells since she was a child. Peter was still sleeping. The weekends were her favourite time as the mill's machinery was silent.

Stopping, she watched a circle of birds that had been disturbed in the woods, only to drop down on the treetops again when the danger had passed. The large black cat that followed her swished its tail against her leg, and Jenny bent down and stroked the furry head.

'What I'd give to soar like those birds,' she whispered. The cat brushed harder against her leg, lifting its head and mewing in sympathy.

Jenny suddenly stretched out her arms, her long fair hair flying behind her as she ran across the field twisting and twirling in a pagan dance.

'Pan Pan,' she called, her face lifted to the woods. 'How I love this land.'

She wasn't addressing her pet but the ancient god of the woodlands who answered with a breeze that swept through the trees and sent back a soft sound; that to a musical person would remind them of a reed instrument.

Something made her direct her attention to one of the small windows in the second floor of the mill and she smiled.

John Tilstone watched Jenny from the mill window, moving back a little into the shadows as she looked up.

'God, how the girl spooked him,' he thought. He never felt so uncomfortable yet more fascinated by anyone else in his life. It was as if she beckoned and repelled him at the same time.

John watched hypnotized as she made for a bend in the riverbank lifting her clothes above her head with each step she took. As the land fell away to the river his view of her became obscured.

He stood transfixed against his will awaiting her reappearance. She knew he was watching he told himself. He wondered if she thought he came to the mill when it was empty just to see her. Normally he would have instigated further involment but now she was just a distraction he didn't need. He needed this time alone to deal with his quandary. Yet up to now the ledger remained unopened on his desk and his body refused to move towards it.

Staring down from the grubby window and hardly breathing John waited till she appeared at last. Her slender white arms lifting her hair up in a veil of sunshine and droplets of water running down her naked body. For a second he could almost feel her tender skin and the softness of her hair, trying at the same time to block out those green eyes that never looked back at you, but through you.

There were times John asked himself why he had not tried his luck with her. He never had any difficulty with the odd mill worker who he trusted to be discrete. Yet Jenny Simkins was different in a way that half frightened him.

Why hadn't the Simkins been relocated when the cottages were condemned he had once asked his wife. There had been no answer; just the shrug of shoulders that constantly reminded him he would never be a Ravenscroft, only the husband of one and therefore it wasn't his business. The overwhelming confidence he had once had from being a lowly manager of the mill to successfully seducing the owner's sister had waned sharply over the last year and it reminded him of the reason he had come here.

Slumping down into the threadbare chair at his desk, he spun around and opened the ledger. A hint of a headache begging to form behind his eyes

Refreshed by the cold water, Jenny's thoughts turned to her next job; the gathering of the herbs that grew in abundance all around. The herbs were sweet at this time. She mustn't forget the watercress for Peter sandwiches. How she loved this land, it gave her all she needed and she knew she would die if she left it.

Why then did she feel apprehensive; she had awoken with the feeling of something about to happen and the feeling wouldn't go away. Even though she had no worries, she had awoken just as dawn was breaking with a need to go to the window and gaze at the fields and woods.

Trust your instincts her mother used to say. The Simkins have always been where they should be, it's only a matter of time. Her mother also told her to listen carefully to the sounds of the woods and make ready when the sound changed. Jenny had instinctively known what she was being told, for the river too had its own song. As a child the gentle breezes across the fields had lulled to sleep. The whole area had a harmony of its own, but knew she was cutely aware of change about to come and she didn't know what. A feeling of foreboding swept through her. She lifted her gaze to the window again, but this time it was empty. She made her way back to cottage in a thoughtful mood.

Chapter 5

John Tilstone stared; sulking at his wife's stiff back as she faced the bay window that overlooked the busy main road.

'Christ John, it's not good enough' she was saying, her voice shrill and impatient. 'This is the third time I've had to attend functions without you.' Her husband slid his long body further into the leather chair and clasped its arms with tense hands. His head and neck felt heavy, the pressure had been building up all day and Kristen's whining was the last thing he needed. He took a deep breath and exhaled slowly. It helped in subduing the frustration that raged within.

Once he had loved this room with its marble fireplace and the handsome furniture that spoke of wealth and breeding. Now he had begun to hate the accusing hooded Ravencroft eyes as they studied him from their portraits. In fact he was beginning to hate "Ravens Nest" itself, the large red brick Victorian house that stood at the top of the mill lane. He had begun to visualise a modern house set back from the road by a long drive in Prestbury, but that would take time and careful handling, especially of Kristen.

She was still talking, her high cultured voice chastising him as she would a schoolboy.

'What were you doing at the mill anyway?' John sat up; he hadn't expected her to ask what he was doing there. 'Machinery complaints from the workers.' He sighed as though he was a victim before adding, 'but you wouldn't understand that nitty-gritty.' Kristen turned slightly so the light caught her face showing the taut shallow skin and high cheekbones, her mouth sculptured into a grim thin line. No amount of makeup could hide the fact she was not pretty or even slightly attractive. Kristen Tilstone was plain to the point of no descriptive. She was nobody's fool and knew only too well she'd managed to catch an attractive man because of her money. But lately she was aware of coming to terms with the fact it was money and not love that kept him by her side. Occasionally the frustration found its voice and leapt out as it did now.

'Don't you dare patronise me. I grew up with the working of the mill and know what it takes to keep the products moving. I am a partner and have to know what's going on. You were just a machinist when we met.' She sniffed, 'I may have been vulnerable with you, but not with the mill.' John hadn't expected this outburst.

Suddenly the tension between them became for him more of a feeling of panic. His only weapon he'd ever had was her obsession with him. Not so long ago he could have twisted her around his little finger just with a touch or attention. Something had changed and it was unsettling him. Careful, be careful; the warning kept passing through his mind.

He sighed the sigh of a parent awaiting the tantrum to end. He got up from the chair with a look of devoted love on his handsome face.

'Darling, oh darling I hurt you. It won't happen again I promise. The trouble is I suppose I'm trying to hard to prove my worth in the family and make you proud of me in my own right.'

He pulled her thin frame towards him, gently stroking her hair and nuzzling her ear. After a moment he felt her relax against him and smiled. She was his, there was no way she could resist him. The confidence returned as he mumbled in her ear about his undying love and loyalty. For a split second, the image of the golf president's wife face came to mind.

'Hush, hush, I promise from now on the mill will take second place to my dearest Kristy.'

She snuggled up to his chest, all her aggravation melting away like snow in the springtime. That's all what she wanted, just him to herself and she had already made a move in that direction. She had already been looking at holiday brochures.

'Let's take a week off darling. There will be no need for further discussion until the accounts are done. Hugo has called in the accountants for a complete assessment of the mill's accounts, so you can relax and let someone else worry about the figures.'

John stiffened, he felt slightly dizzy and breathless. Holding his wife tightly against him, he tried to get possession of his wits.

'When are you picking up the books?' He asked, trying to sound nonchalant and unconcerned, while releasing her at the same time and making for the liquor cabinet.

'Two weeks I believe. Sherry for me John, please.'

Whisky in one hand and sherry in the other, John handing his wife her glass before settling himself back in the leather chair, 'and what brought that on?' he asked.

'Partly my fault, I like to check the figures now and then.' She looked at her husband over her glass; the gaze steady and unflinching.

John took a deep drink; the fiery liquid burning is throat. He wished desperately she would go. Christ, he couldn't handle it if she got amorous now. The thought sickened him and he winced out loud.

'Something wrong?' She was looking at him and he swore she had a quiet smile on her face like someone who had hooked a large fish.

'My idea of course, bringing in the accountants,' said Kristen. 'Hugo wasn't too keen and didn't think it necessary, but it's as well to keep a check on the figures don't you think dear.' John nodded; the show of hands a blind to his true feelings. 'Of course it could be left. Maybe there really isn't any need. Perhaps we should have a nice holiday in Spain before thinking of business. What do you think?'

Twice she'd asked for his opinion. Something was not right. For one thing she never asked his advice and secondly she was holding her gaze for longer than normal. John's reaction was the total opposite to what he felt, but he prided himself on knowing women, especially his wife.

'Ah well that's something I think I could handle. A holiday.' He made himself appear full of enthusiasm.

'Yes just you and me on a beach, in sunny Spain with no worries. Who would want to think of accounts before or even after?' he added.

He leaned forward and raised his glass. 'To us in Spain then.'

'To us.' A chink of glassware followed her response.

'No Accountants?'

'No; not at this time.'

John watched her as she sank back against the brown leather, making her skin and hair pasty and mouse-like. His imagination dare not go to bikinis and beaches, at least not with her figuring in it. Time, time was all that was needed and life could take a turn for the better. Suddenly he felt back in charge, his two feet planted solidly on firm ground, as he liked to say. Apart that was, from a nagging little feeling his wife was still holding all the cards. Time will tell as his dad used to say, and John fully agreed with the sentiment.

The phone rang. Kristen jumped up and made for the hall. John listened to some mumbling and a couple of high-pitched laughs, then silence broken only by the flick of a page being lifted and turned.

'Someone for Hugo.' Kristen entered the room and moved over to the sherry bottle, holding it up to the light to read the label on it, followed by a slight look of dismay. 'Who brought this cheap stuff?' John's fingers curled up into fists, there was always some criticism. She knew full well who had brought it.

Chapter 6

The first warm rays of the morning sun danced over the tops of the yellow daffodils that covered Gelsby's village green. The villagers hurried to form groups and gossip awhile before the church bells stopped ringing and the worshipers from further away circled the green before finding a parking space.

The small space allotted to the church was already jammed with vehicles; the parishioners had turned a blind eye to the no-parking signs outside their cottages. As long as St Anne's pews and coffers were filled they found little to complain about for one day of the week.

This sunny morning saw the ancient church pews well occupied, which had become quite usual after the tragic deaths of the last rector and his sister. It was as though a new loyalty had emerged, letting the outsiders know the church would remain when all else collapsed, as it had done since the thirteenth century and been witness to many a tragedy over the intervening years.

Inside the same sun streamed through the beautiful stained glass window depicting the life and times of Jesus Christ; its small pieces of coloured glass producing patterns of colour around the altar. Halfway down the left-hand side of the red-carpeted aisle sat Hugo Ravenscroft and his sister Kristen, her handsome husband duly noted as missing by the regulars. John had pleaded the beginning of a migraine, which hadn't convinced his wife of the truth of it at all.

Kristen sat bolt upright, her hands clasped tightly on her lap. She stared straight ahead tracing the intricatecarving of the rood screen, in a desperate effort to keep her anger under control. Did he think she was stupid? Who did he think he was? This wasn't the first time she would have to make excuses to the Hatton's, who had invited them to lunch. It would mean she had to make small talk and laugh at their silly jokes, today of all days, when her mind was on more important things. She was also angry with her brother as well, for informing her too late of his prior arrangements.

She felt Hugo's impatience to get the service over with. Nothing was said, but it was something she had always been sensitive to.

Over the other side and further to the rear of the church Lisa sat between Ernest and Ted struggling to maintain a resemblance of composure. Lisa's thoughts kept drifting back to a few weeks ago when she had parked her mother's wheelchair by the last pew at the back of the church.

A tear ran down her cheek; she sniffed and then gave a little cough. A large hand laid itself over hers and gave it a little squeeze. Glancing up she looked to her old gov's steady gaze and managed to smile. It was nice to know Ernest understood, yet underneath wished it had been Ted that had recognised her need. She moved her position slightly towards him hoping for something that would tell her he too was a support. Ted was flicking over the pages of her hymnbook, his own already opened and just waiting to be picked up at the first sound of the music. Briefly Lisa wondered if he would have found Ernest's page also if he could have reached over to it.

For a second she experienced an uncontrollable urge to laugh, but had rendered it harmless with another little cough. Suddenly the organ came to life with the choir and rector following the cross and candle bearers filing in procession down the aisle.

The form of the service had not been changed to the more modern version by the previous two rectors and had brought no challenges from the congregation. The dioceses had thought it fit to remain with the conservative side of the service when electing the new rector to the parish; a small non-descript of a man with pale skin and watery eyes, but blessed with a clear and pleasant voice.

No one could have guessed that the fair-haired young man sitting by his sister's side was in a world far away from the sermon now being delivered. His thoughts were solely on Jenny Simkins and what he was going to say to her. Hugo straightened out his arm so the sleeve rode up showing his watch. Not long now, this time he had to remain firm and deal with his problems.

Half an hour later, the congregation was trickling out of St. Anne's, stopping as usual to pass niceties with the new rector and then to collect in groups to gossip.

'Are you sure you can't make it?' Kristen asked, the disappointment she had perfected over the years written all over her face.

'Sorry, give my regrets.' Hugo didn't look around. Closing the car door with a bang he took off; his thoughts troubled.

God he hoped the boy wasn't there. Explaining to Jenny was enough without the boy's soulful eyes studying him. Before he knew it he was turning past Ravens Nest and entering Mill Lane, totally unaware that he was being watched from an upstairs window of the big house, the watcher giving time for the car to disappear before fetching out a cycle from the outside shed and following it.

Hugo parked in the mill yard, and then made his way towards the occupied cottage. Pushing open the iron gate, he walked towards the open back door.

Humming was coming from the kitchen, a low tuneless hum that made him uncomfortable and apprehensive. Although he'd known her all his life, she still unnerved him with her humming.

'Get a grip,' Hugo told himself; straightening his back as if going into battle.

'Jenny.' He entered the small room, momentarily being taken aback as she spun around, fear written all over her face.

'Peter?' he asked.

'Out,' her voice was barely a whisper.

Hugo pulled out a chair and sat at the bare scrub-topped table, his hands spread before him. Better come straight to the point. He took a deep breath.

'I want you to move out of here.' He hesitated before adding, 'Peter and you, I want you to move . . .'

Nothing. There was no response. The air hung still with a faint smell of herbs along with the now chilling silence. Now he could feel himself getting exasperated and annoyed. Why did she always go silent when he needed to be in charge of the situation? He recalled the same treatment when he'd suggested the child was not his.

The silence was worse than crying, pleading to any of the emotions that he could muster to start the flow of his adrenaline. But with nothing to hit against, his anger departed.

'No.'

'What?' Hugo sat up and stared at her.

'No Hugo.' Jenny turned her back on him and started to stir the pot that was simmering on the stove.

'I can make you, the cottage can be condemned.' Suddenly he felt powerful and in control. 'All I have to do is get an order to say the place is unfit to bring up a child in. The water for one thing, the pipes are all lead and the toilet is still outside.'

'We are not moving Hugo, and that's that. You are free to marry and Peter is mine and mine alone. But I warn you if you threaten us I will go as far as a DNA test to prove who his father is . . .' she paused before adding, 'and what age was I; when you raped me.'

A cold sweat had begun to spread over Hugo. He tried to appear calm and in control offering a very sensible and workable solution.

'I am willing to buy you a house.' He stopped, sliding his hand across the table in a gesture of goodwill. 'Not big I admit, but one you and Peter could live comfortably in and . . .' He waited for the expected look on her face, but when it didn't appear he added. 'A modest amount would be paid into the bank until the boy comes of age. No questions; just a steady income.'

'And what would Kristen and John have to say to that?' The question was sharp and half-mocking.

'They won't know, I'll have the accountants in next week, and arrange the books to compensate. They'll do it; anything can be done for a price.'

'Can it?' Jenny's voice had an edge to it, yet her expression had not changed.

'What do you say Jenny?'

Hugo twitched suddenly and looked towards the door as a sound of something falling was heard. Jenny stiffened, her hearing acute, then just as suddenly she relaxed, a wisp of a smile crossing her face.

'Jenny, come on, what do you say, we will both benefit and can put the past behind us, and I can't be fairer than that. I was young and not used to drink.' His voice took on a pleading vain; the anxiety evident in its tone.

Jenny turned down the heat on the stove and brought a chair to the table. Quietly she took his hands in hers and looked at the weak but handsome face.

'Ah Hugo, I regret nothing. Peter is all I want. Now, the world spins and like a ball of wool, the yarn weaves and intertwines. Everything gets played out in time. Lifetimes are nothing; it's the seeds that eventually bare the fruit of the past wrongs and only in time do those things get righted. We are but parts of that yarn.'

Hugo sat quite still, unable to move, her voice both mesmerising and holding him in suspense. For one brief moment he experienced something primitive, some force he didn't understand yet knew he was part of. Then it was gone and reality reigned. Pulling back his hands, he asked again for the answer he needed.

'Ah Jenny I don't want to start any trouble for you, but one day I would like to get married and start clean like.'

She closed her eyes and when she opened them she wore a far away look.

'Jenny, what do you say?'

'Do what you have to do.' There was genuine sorrow in her voice as she said it. Nothing will stop what was started long ago.

Hugo sighed, Jenny was a strange woman but he would wear her down in time.

Chapter 7

A pair of sunken blue eyes set into a pale shallow face stared back at Lisa. She opened her mouth sticking out a white-coated tongue before giving a slight shudder and sighing. Opening the bathroom mirrored medicine cabinet Lisa replaced a small bottle containing sleeping pills. Although her doctor had prescribed them a week ago, last night was the first time she had taken any.

This morning she felt a lot better apart from being slightly sluggish which she knew would pass as time wore on. The other thing she felt easier about was at last coming to terms with her mother's funeral.

Lisa ran the cold-water tap and splashed her face. Her face in the mirror now appeared brighter with colour in the cheeks. One step at a time Ernest had said, and this morning she felt ready to take the first steps of her new life without her mother.

It would do her the world of good to spend a day on Ted's farm.

'Nothing like good old fresh air to clear away the vapours,' her mother would have said, so when Ted suggested she should visit, she agreed.

The morning's weather had turned out good, despite Ted's predictions of rain in the air, which gave Lisa a sense of satisfaction she couldn't explain.

Warm enough for a light coat though, Lisa thought.

Although feeling more refreshed as time moved on, she now thought it best take a brolly; as Ted was usually right. He often reminded her that being close to the earth one gets to know when the weather is in for a change.' No need for scientists to tell me about global warming, I could have told them years ago,' he'd said; giving her that self-satisfied look she found so irritating. But one couldn't really fault him for that. When he predicted rain; it rained.

Today Lisa decided against finding fault and to start looking only for the positives in life. She'd lost her aging mother, which she'd told Ernest was only to be expected; given her age, but then regretted her new positive outlook on life when she caught his pained look in return; him being not too far off her mother's age.

'One mistake mustn't keep oneself from taking steps towards a new life,' she'd told herself afterwards. What could be nicer than being totally in tune with nature; eating the produce of the land or watching the newborn lambs and calves, as would be the case on Ted's land.

'Gives you a good appetite,' Ted had said, but it always left Lisa wondering who would be doing the cooking.

By mid-morning Lisa was on her way to the farm, when she remembered her trash bin should have gone out to be collected. Giving a curse under her breath, she gave her steering wheel a mighty tug to the right spinning the vehicle around in the narrow lane, missing by inches a car that had appeared from around the bend. Slamming on the brakes, she was aware of a horn sounding and her heart pumping loudly in her ears.

Christ, what was she thinking of? If there had been an accident, it would have cost her her job. The pounding in her chest slowed down as Lisa convinced herself that the sleeping pills were to blame.

Having deposited the trash bin along side a row of them by the church's parking ground, she set off again. This time she was fully concentrated and followed the road alongside the old church wall towards Belton, turning off at the crossroads along a narrower road that cut a straight line between the flat green pasture lands of the Cheshire plains. Each parcel of land divided by hedges; usually hawthorn, which was now in flower. Occasionally oak trees harboured patches of yellow wild flowers where the cows stood, swishing the flies away with their tails and looking dumb and contented.

From the plains arose the last of the hills of the Pennine Chain or the backbone of England, as it was often referred to. Here it ended in a shape that the locals referred to as the Giant's Foot, although the Roman fortification that once stood there would have had its own name no doubt. Farms were dotted here and there, all older than the turn of the eighteenth century, with one of them still with its thatched roof and dug well.

Green's farm could not be missed, even without Ted's carefully written instructions. A large sign by the entrance gave the owner's name and breed of cows, with a smaller "Please close the gate" instruction, well placed on the gate.

Opening and closing the gate was no effort. It seemed to swing into position with ease. The muddy drive however seemed long with only the tops of the buildings showing over the rolling land. Lisa manoeuvred the ruts cursing at every bump till the farm came into sight. Her dreams of a pretty farmhouse surrounded by flowering blossoms immediately vanished. Here was an old stone structure, surrounded by lofty barns and fenced places where cows and pigs wallowed in mud.

A large black and white collie came bounding towards her car, leaping up and barking in excitement as she opened the door. A man was emerging from the barn and it took a few moments for Lisa to recognise Ted in overly large overalls and mud spattered boots.

'You're late.'

Lisa coughed and tried hard to retain a sense of humour.

'What for, milking the cows?' She'd obviously hit the spot first time; but he wasn't laughing.

'Milking won't wait like the arresting of criminals.' There was criticism in his voice as he came nearer. If Lisa had expected open arms and a quick kiss she didn't get either; just a nod towards the house and a dismissal. 'Susan will see to you.'

Ted turned and walked to the cowshed, leaving Lisa to guess who Susan was, but then realised there had been three of them all the time. Leaning by the door was a tall thin girl about Lisa's age; ginger hair tied up in a ponytail, a face covered in freckles and red patches caused by exposure to the weather. She too was dressed for farm work; stained jeans and an old tee shirt. She didn't move as Lisa approached her, just stood there appraising her like a new heifer.

Lisa smiled and tried to look in control.

'You're Susan?'

The girl nodded and stepped aside to let Lisa pass. A faint but recognisable smell emanated from the girl. Lisa coughed again.

To Lisa's surprise, the kitchen was large and as neat as a new pin. A large Agar stove stood to one side. The pile of logs next to it looked as if each one had been carefully cut to size. Susan started to fold some laundry, before lifting down an old duffle coat from behind the back door.

'I'm off then, stew's in the pot.' She glanced over at the stove before letting her eyes rest on Lisa. 'Just as Ted likes it, he will be back in two hours.'

The girl left, leaving Lisa a little bewildered and angry.

'Will he indeed.' She spoke out loud to herself, 'and what the frigging hell am I to do till then.'

Energy mounting from her frustration, she decided it was too a nice day to sit watching the pot simmer, after all a farm should have nicer things than cows and pigs. There must be hens and maybe a duck pond with some nice friendly white ducks.

As soon as she stepped outside, Lisa knew her choice of shoes was wrong. The mud seemed to find its way up the sides and into the shoes themselves. Bending down she examined the mud more closely. It seemed too light a brown and had bits of straw in it. A sudden squawk and a mass of feathers leapt at her.

'Stupid hens,' she muttered.

Lisa walked over to the fence overlooking a field of long grass and leaned against it. Somehow it looked neglected and she immediately felt an aversion to it.

'What the hell had she come for?' She told herself and gritted her teeth till she felt the pressure on her gums. 'The bloody dog has more attention.'

Ted sometimes reminded her of two very different people; the pleasant guy with twinkling eyes that wanted to do everything and the one that was sullen and distant if he was displeased. Well if anyone seemed to understand him Susan did. There was little doubt that the girl doted on him. Who the heck was she anyway? Ted had never mentioned her. Here she was a good detective in her own right and she was at a loss for answers.

'The field's fallowing.' Lisa jumped; her nerves already on edge. A man in his sixties and dressed for farm work leaned on the gate by her side. 'You be Emily's girl then?' The question came across as more of a statement. 'Mighty sorry to hear she's passed on.' The voice was local and genuine in sympathy. Lisa nodded. 'Susan's me daughter.' He had all the answers without having been asked any questions. 'Helped here with my Alice before she passed away. Good girl she is, and loves the farm.'

His head turned slightly and Lisa knew he was watching her.

'Ted tells me you will be giving up thy job at the Police Department when thar comes here permanent like, hope thee are good with cows.'

Lisa's throat began to tighten, leaving her wanting to cough and unable to do so. Instead she just cleared her throat.

The man gazed over the fields again. 'Not everyone understands Ted. Once he's made up his mind to do something or have something done, it sets like concrete in his head; if thar knows what I mean.'

Lisa instinctively knew he was warning her in his own way without being offensive, and she'd played the game like her job had taught her to.

'It's best if I learn to fit in so to speak, and not to question too much like.'

'Aye lass, something likes that.'

'One boss?'

'Aye, one boss.'

'Susan sees it like that, does she?'

'Aye she does, just like her Ma before her.'

Lisa continued to hold her gaze across the field, yet well aware the farm worker had moved away. She surprised herself on how she felt. Certainly not compromised anymore, but relieved that what she felt had been said.

Was Ted really the one for her? All she knew was she didn't want to go through life alone, but what was the alternative?

She looked back towards the house, then past it to her car.

It was the second one she made for.

Driving home, the let-down feeling never materialised. Instead a wave of release seemed to sweep over her body and new energy began to seep into every crevice of her being. She switched her cell phone off and turned into the lane at the rear of her house. Instead of opening her back door she opened Ernest's. She felt in need of a good cup of tea and a natter. Farms weren't really her thing; whether Ted was she would think on that later.

Chapter 8

Professor Thomas Reece wished he had been more selective in his accommodation and had not taken it on a recommendation. Standing by the window, he looked over the rooftops and lush green foliage of trees beneath him. He hadn't known at the time that the hotel was situated on the edge of the town, not that the view could be faulted in any way. At this early hour of the morning the scenery offered a tranquillity all its own. He could see the river quite clearly and the new overpass that took the traffic away from the town centre. He couldn't fault the food either, a little over-the-top in presentation maybe, but nevertheless extremely tasty. In fact he'd over indulged himself over dinner the night before, by having ice cream with the raspberry pie.

However there was one problem that frustrated him. Although the walk into the town was downhill, the return journey was far from inviting as the Saxon Arms was built on the top of a high incline. Tom sighed and wondered if he should enquire about the buses, if in fact the town ran a bus transport service at all. A lot of places didn't anymore.

The map he had with him showed that the main street of the town was closed to traffic. That happened a lot in the older towns that wished to keep their history and had recognised that the existing thoroughfare was far too narrow to accommodate present-day traffic. Tom didn't object to that, in fact he was in full agreement. The truth was it was his bike he missed, having never acquired a driving license and never intending to. His bicycle with its large basket on the front got him around his university town quite nicely, and public transport did the job for the bigger journeys.

What with his careful planning of what to do and see, he felt quite let down. He shouldn't trust anyone to see to his needs, especially his accommodation. He hadn't mentioned he had no transport of his own. Now he felt restricted and annoyed, vowing to change his accommodation once his contact had been to see him.

An aeroplane flew overhead, its vapour trail rapidly disappearing behind it. He watched it for a few seconds trying to think where he'd heard one could tell the coming weather by the stability of such a trail left by a plane. Nothing came to mind. Letting the curtain fall back in place, he walked over to the bed and sat down so heavily that the springs protested by creaking.

He had made the bed himself, its counterpane crisply folded and the pillows puffed up. A neat man, it annoyed him to await a maid to set the room to rights. At the foot of the bed lay a big bundle of files all neatly arranged in the order of what they pertained to. The pile marked Ravenscroft had scattered as he had sat down. Tom stared at them blankly. Is this the end of the journey? he pondered. There was a strange emptiness he'd never experienced before. This is what had obsessed him all his life and now____. His visualisation couldn't comprehend it; there seemed no future.

His obsession had begun so long ago he now couldn't recall his actual age when it all happened. He knew he was still young at the time, for it was before his grandfather had died. That moment of discovering witches existed and were not fairy tales, had changed his life and had charted his future career. The day he discovered the old dusty chest in his grandfather's house and had read the papers of Matthew Hopkins, England's Witchfinder General, he was captivated to know all he could about his ancestors.

He read every word of the trials and the substance of the sentences, not only reading them but as an impressionable child living them in his imagination. However one trial had really got to him and as a result, it became vital for him to right an old wrong.

Tom had read Matthew Hopkins's papers about the trials and the personal wealth gained.

The consequence of finding the papers had led to Tom reading history and becoming a professor; his knowledge and enthusiasm for his subject making his lectures well attended. However where other successful men would have sought a life of married bliss and children, Tom's thoughts were fully occupied with research and one particular witch's death.

Then one day quite of the blue, but not without help from the powers that be in Tom's mind, he'd picked up an article entitled "The Silk Mills of Cheshire". It told about the Ravencroft family, who had owned a mill and adjoining lands for over three hundred and fifty years, and of their decision in the early eighteen hundreds to transform the old water wheel driven mill into a progressive engineering company to support the silk industry; the manager John Tilstone now saying it was doing extremely well.

Could this be a coincidence? Ravencroft and Simkins and their families might still exist in the same location. Tom was beside himself and threw himself into researching their ancestry from church records and available censuses. To his amazement he found the offsprings of the families were indeed still around. Such was his excitement that his retirement was totally devoted to charting every line of the family trees and he discovered the families were still on the same land.

The anxiety and excitement wouldn't let his mind rest. He was ready and he needed to see at last a face that had genes of the people he'd lived and thought about for so long.

Why hadn't the telephone rung? He glanced over to it and stopped as his eyes settled on the clock. He groaned.

'Six thirty.' It was his fault. He was too eager, yet he knew it was no use thinking of sleeping again. He tried to think of the stocks that still remained in the old market place where Beth Simkins was held for a day and night without food or water.

Tom imagined as he'd done hundreds of times before, the shaving of Beth's hair that cut her scalp and causing the many flies and other insects around the market place to settle and feast on the oozing and congealing blood. He'd asked himself a real life question.

'What happened when her bladder or bowels needed relieving?' those little normal things taken so much for granted. She would be soiled; her excrements running down her legs, her throat burning with thirst, her stomach hollow. Then there were the witch-prickers with their pins and needles; plodding and probing her tender flesh for witch's marks to see if they bled. The knowledge of her agony that his ancestor had ordered and watched fulfilled; left Tom with a horror he couldn't overcome.

The phone rang. Tom stared at it at first as though it was an intrusion into his inner self, but then leapt up to grab the instrument.

'Yes.' He became aware he was shouting and quickly lowered his excitement. 'Yes,' he repeated.

'I'm here, what's your number?' The voice was soft and almost a whisper.

'Number forty two___, second floor.'

'Open your door; I'll be there in a minute.' The phone went silent.

Scrambling across the room, Tom unlatched the door and peered down the corridor. It was silent and empty; the wrong time of the year for there to be many occupants. Leaving the door slightly open as instructed, he fussed over the files, leaving them in strict order of reference. His excitement knew no bounds; at least the past and future were now coming together.

He felt a presence before he turned and when he did he was surprised at the figure observing him.

'So you are the professor that cannot leave the dead alone.' The visitor's voice was neither teasing nor offensive, just a factual statement. However Tom found himself blushing.

'I suppose I am,' he confessed, still taking in the presence that had now closed the door of the room.

'Is that it?' Tom looked over at the bed and nodded. 'All of it?' the question sounded more like a comment and the professor began to feel a discomfort in the pit of his stomach, but managed to answer with enthusiasm.

'Yes, it's the records of both families for three hundred years and more.'

There was a short sniff followed by a hollow laugh before the voice took on a sarcastic overtone.

'You are as mad as the Witchfinder, although he probably did make more of a profit than you.'

The professor's face paled and stiffened, he hadn't expected to be confronted with criticism over his life's work. Somewhere in the recesses of his brain he heard his father's voice rebuking him over his obsession with the past.

He opened his mouth to say something in his defence, but the words were never uttered as something caught his eye that glinted then whipped past in a downward stroke. A sharp cut followed by an excruciating pain in his neck. He tried to cry out to express the torment, but nothing would manifest itself. Only his fading sense of hearing picked up a gurgling sound and there was taste of blood in his mouth. Then he was falling down into blackness with nothing to hold him. The pain receded as he hit the side of his head on the bed table.

A blood stained knife was placed swiftly into a plastic bag. It hadn't been as difficult as was thought. The papers were gathered up and slipped into a bigger bag with the wrapped weapon. A quick check around the room and another down the corridor for early risers and the mission was accomplished.

Chapter 9

Lying alone in her bedroom on the morning of the funeral, Lisa stared into the dark. There wasn't a shaft of light from the open curtains. Outside the night was pitch black, not one single star to give any reference to the exterior.

Tonight no tablets had been taken to bring on sleep; that veil with its blessed oblivion. She didn't want it. This was her time to be with her memories and the presence of her mother's spirit.

Lisa straightened her body out, her arms and hands stiff by her sides. She needed to feel the solitude of death. Relaxing her body to the point of non-feeling, Lisa found herself detached from her physical being. It was as if she was standing back looking at her own body. Was death like this she wondered? Maybe in death the body and mind play no part; leaving the spirit to observe without attachment to its former self. Taking a deep breath, Lisa tried to let her thoughts go and just watch the process without emotion.

Then a terrible ache grew in her chest, which became too heavy and had to be released through a bout of sobbing. Tears ran unabashed down her cheeks.

'Oh mum, where have you gone?'

Then as quickly as the emotion found its outlet, it subsided and she thought of Jiten, his pleasant dusky brown face floating from her subconscious and recalling hearing his compassionate nature and words he had spoken. "Reincarnation means there is no real death; the spirit just takes on another vehicle to purify itself."

Lisa remembered she had rolled her eyes up in her head; it was a hard concept to accept after being brought up in the Church of England tradition of heaven and hell. Now she regretted making fun of him and asked him with a straight face if he thought she'd joined the police force out of a need for justice. He'd nodded, but then looked downcast as she shook her head and had added very seriously, 'No Jiten, you're wrong. I joined for the uniform.'

Lisa, lifted the bed-sheet, stuck it between her teeth and bit hard. What makes her like that?

Light was now drifting into the bedroom. She turned towards her bedside table. Eight-thirty a.m. A sound of a car followed; she listened to it slowing down, a car door slammed shut followed by a rattle at her own front door.

'Oh God, I forgot,' was her first thought; sitting up so quickly, it left her feeling a little bit disoriented. 'Ted!'

Two minutes later, her dressing gown pulled together like a sack and tied with a piece of cord she pulled back the door bolt. Ted still had his finger on the bell and looked put out.

'I told you to let me get a key cut.' He pushed passed her, stopping to adjust his black tie in front of the hall mirror. 'The car will be here at ten sharp, don't you think you should shower and get ready?'

'Bugger off,' Lisa muttered to herself as she climbed the stairs wondering at the same time why hadn't he said anything about her behaviour at the farm.

Half way up the stairs she regretted the thought. After all he'd made all the arrangements for her, even to the type of wood for the coffin, and was being sympathetic to her erratic behaviour now. He'd taken a lot of stress away even to advising her to have no flowers, arranging instead for donations to the Heart and Stroke Foundation. She didn't disagree at the time, but now had a niggling thought her mother would have liked flowers, especially freshly cut ones.

Ted was talking to Ernest when she eventually reappeared. She'd already imagined a look of impatience on Ted's face for taking such a long drawn out bath time and was in no way hurrying; telling herself after all her mum wasn't going anywhere fast. This thought brought on a feeling of shame at her own flippancy as she remembered the effort and kindness so many of the villagers had put into making it a special farewell for one of their own. Ted's face portrayed an appreciation at her choice of a smart black suit and delicately heeled shoes. Even though it was the worst day of her life, Lisa had to agree with Ted when she saw her own image in the hall mirror.

Ernest's face on the other hand reflected nothing but the sympathy the occasion demanded.

'Ready love' he quizzed, holding out his crooked arm for her to hold. Ted looked put out, but had little choice in the matter except to follow, as the chief mourners stepped outside to the car waiting to follow the hearse. Most of the other mourners had walked and the whole village seemed to be making for St. Anne's; not really surprising as most of them had known Emily Pharies all their lives.

Lisa's hand found Ernest's and clutched it tightly, as the coffin was placed on a trolley and wheeled in before them. Now the kneeling for private prayer, she felt numb and distanced from everything. Then she was standing, having been lifted by Ernest's strong arm.

The new rector was standing before the coffin and he was speaking about Emily Pharies. Lisa wondered where he had got his information from but had only to see the confirming look on Ted's face to know. She wasn't angry and thought it rather nice someone cared. A sudden affection arose for him from within as she realised again, he had never reprimanded her for leaving the farm without an explanation. He probably understood, and that was a comforting feeling for her.

Her old school teacher was pounding out her mother's favourite hymn on the organ. Lisa noticed the wrinkled stocking her teacher was wearing and it helped keep an emotional lump from forming in her chest as she watched the wrinkles moving in time with the music.

Soon the service was over and, to the strains of "The Lord is my Shepherd", they filed quietly out into the sunshine to follow the funeral cortège to the new graveyard further away from the church. The air was warm, and it seemed to brighten everyone's spirits and tongues, creating a background of muffled voices as they followed the coffin along the narrow graveyard path.

Then at last Lisa was standing before the open grave. She experienced a momentary numbness again as though she was fading away.

Ernest put his arm around her as she swayed, and kept it there throughout the burial service.

'It's all over' he said quietly, 'let her go in peace love.' She nodded and smiled through her tear filled eyes at those that gave only glimpses of quiet understanding. Stooping she gathered a handful of earth and scattered it over the wooden coffin that held her mother.

Suddenly the pain was too much to stay unrecognized and nothing could have stopped the cry that followed. It sounded like an animal in distress. She heard Ted whisper; "hush" which only seemed to activate her trembling. Suddenly she was being pulled to a large warm chest and a white handkerchief was being stuffed into her hand.

'Have a good blow,' came the command.

She did as she was told, looked up at the brooding eyes under heavy eyebrows and wanted to cry again, but held it in as she peered over the hankie at the people around.

Over by another grave that sported a large stone angel and red and white artificial flowers, she spotted a group of her colleagues from the Police Station. They were deep in conversation and occasionally one or other would look her way. Ted took her elbow and was by this time edging her away.

'People need refreshments,' he reminded her. 'Let's go.' She looked at him bewildered for a second, but then began gathering up the last of her energy reserves.

Ernest watched them go, then turned as a voice behind him uttered,

'She's tougher than what she seems, you know,' before adding, 'she'll be alright.' The voice belonged to Dr. Jeremiah Potts, the family doctor. As the two men walked through the graveyard towards the old church hall, Ernest looked up at the ancient church as they passed and sighed. 'If only walls could talk.'

The doctor stopped, his gaze travelling upwards. 'Yes indeed,' he said understandingly. 'They must have more to tell than our history books, I guess.'

Suddenly Ernest remembered it being said that the doctor was somewhat of an expert on Cheshire history, and his thoughts flashed back to an earlier conversation he had had on the train.

'I know this sounds silly but were there any cases of witch-burning around here?' The doctor stopped, leaving Ernest to turn around and wait for his companion.

'Where's that question coming from? In all my years of delving into the county's history, I've never been asked that before.'

Ernest laughed adding; 'Well this village has seen nearly everything else. I just wondered.'

'Well yes; the town did have one case of a witch in the 1700s, but they were always taken to Chester to be burnt. Most were strangled and their bodies brought back and placed on a gibbet on the heath.'

'Heath,' Ernest caught his name and couldn't think along any other lines.

'Yes, Gelsby Heath man.' The doctor laughed. 'In fact that's where pieces of wood from it have since been found there and are now in the local museum.'

Ernest shuddered; Gelsby Heath was the land just across the road from Gelsby. Mostly fields now and where an old hospital once stood; built to house those with infectious diseases like smallpox and diphtheria.

'So what did our witch do to get burnt?' Ernest had to understand if the crime was really tailored to fit the punishment, even if it was over three hundred years ago.

'Seems the young lass married well, and then was accused of killing her husband.'

Ernest's step measured the doctor's as they made their way across the road.

'What a way to die though.' stated Ernest, never in favour of capital punishment.

'Better than being hung, drawn and quartered.' came the reply.

'Christ.' Ernest thought justice had come a long way since then, but then rejected such thoughts with shame, as he reflected on the mistrials that still went on in this day and age.

'Even so, she did curse her accusers,' the doctor added with a tiny smile.

'I'd do the same I guess.' Ernest laughed, though it didn't come that light-heartedly.

'It is surprising how many folk around here still believe in the old ways and superstitions. A couple of years ago I was called out to a woman, whose lad had drowned in the Gelsby Mere; she insisted Nelly Longarms had pulled him in.'

'Nelly Longarms?' Ernest had missed that one completely and wondered if his memory was going.

'Come on Ernest, you've lived around here all your life and pretend you never heard of the water fairy that preys on children. Nelly Longarms is the death fairy that drowns them.'

Ernest looked dumbstruck and almost felt illiterate for not knowing. Jeremiah caught the look and went on with his explanations.

'The Simkins family living by the mill were always clever with herbs.' Having said that he coughed as the pollen from the trees caught the breeze. 'Saw young Jenny only this morning; she was on the heights looking for Baldens broom.' He saw Ernest's mystified look and went on to explain. 'The branches keep mice away from hanging meat. Jenny sells it to farmers.'

'What about fridges?' Ernest asked in disbelief.

'Old ideas take a long time to go away in the country. Do you know I still get grandmothers rubbing their gold rings on their grandchildren's sties?'

'Worked for me.' Ernest said solemnly, before stepping aside to let the doctor enter the church hall first.

Chapter 10

'Fancy taking a walk?' Ernest asked; tucking Lisa's arm under his and giving it a pat. She nodded and falling into step; matched his long strides with ease. They headed off towards the quiet country lane that circled the village of Gelsby. The air was chilly but almost felt invigorating after the stuffy church hall and offered much needed energy to their bodies.

It was a long time before their silence was broken, as it had served as a quiet reflection on the day's happenings. Eventually Ernest said the only word he could think of with out seeming to intrude.

'OK?' he asked, without looking at her.

'Hmm,' she replied, but it was enough for Ernest to know all was well.

The silence continued again, until number eleven was reached. Ernest stopped; one hand on the gate.

'Cuppa?' he asked; indicating with his head towards the door . . .

Lisa nodded and followed him through the gate; its creaking frightened her scruffy marmalade cat that was following them along the side of the path. Lisa gave it a gentle tap on its rump with her shoe and watched its tail disappearing into the overgrown bushes on the opposite side.

Once inside the house she felt the chill seeping through her bones, she shivered and wrapped her arms around herself. Ernest was quick to notice and made some remark about only having to leave the house for a week or so and the damp settles in.

Two minutes later, he was bending down by the gas fire and, switching it on he straightened up before facing her with his hands behind his back. He stood warming them and rubbing his buttocks 'til he caught Lisa's eye and quickly moved away saying something about popping on the kettle.

Lisa lowered herself down into Ernest's favourite chair. A great weariness over came her and she didn't have the strength to fight it. Wrapped in the security of Ernest's presence and mutual understanding, she fell into a deep sleep.

She awoke with a start, not recognizing her surroundings at first and Ernest sitting opposite, watching her with his broody eyes.

'Better?' he asked.

She nodded and yawned

The phone rang.

Lisa reached into her pocket pulling out her cell phone, and then closed it with a click as she indicated the call came from the phone in the hall. She winked at Ernest and waved him away. Ernest had disappeared before she could draw another breath.

'Lucky bastard,' she mused, stretching out her legs and contemplating the ladder in her nylons that ran from toe to knee. She heard him put down the phone, the call had taken less than five minutes. Lisa assumed the cost of transatlantic calls could take a hammering on pensions, especially police ones and Rita was always thrifty.

She sighed: Why couldn't she find the perfect mate like this pair? She heard footsteps returning. A smile started to form, then froze quickly on her lips as she noticed his expression.

'What's up?' Lisa sat up stiff and straight, her gaze defying any excuses for her grieving.

'That was the chief superintendant enquiring about you.'

'Nice of Wiggy,' she remarked sarcastically; using the nickname of Chief Superintendant Wigfull, then recognizing the tone and hesitation in Ernest's voice, said quietly. 'Go on.'

Ernest walked over to the fire taking all the heat again. She didn't say anything; just waited patiently for whatever had brought a soft glint to his eye.

'I have to tell you first that Wiggy said you could take all the time you need to___,' he hesitated, searching for the right word, before adding; 'recover, but.'

Lisa coughed. She was getting annoyed.

'Spit it out Ernest, do you think I'm that daft to think the super would enquire about my health?' Suddenly stopping, she blurted out, 'something has happened in my department hasn't it?'

'Lisa lass, the world can go on without us. There are others that can be brought in.'

'Ernest.' her words exploded in frustration. Ernest rubbed his eyes; it stopped him looking straight at her.

'There's been a body found in a room at the Saxon Hotel; discovered this morning by the maid,' again he hesitated before adding, 'throat cut.'

'Good God.' she tilted her head backwards against the chair and let out a long breath. Then for one uncomfortable moment she visualized Aston, her cousin in his dog collar shaking his head at her choice of words. She coughed and sat up.

Ernest was now settled across from her again leaning back and searching the ceiling. He thought well when he had a white canvas to play his images on, although truth to tell at this moment he was playing for time. He knew Lisa; he'd trained her. At last his patience was rewarded.

'What did you tell him?' asked Lisa. Ernest looked baffled; 'about me, you twit.'

Before he could answer the phone rang again, this time it was her mobile. Ernest watched Lisa's face with interest as she struggled to get it to her ear as fast as she could. He saw colour warming her skin and the eyes appeared to brighten with interest. Then just as quickly the colour drained and Lisa was clearing the nervous spasm that was building in her throat.

'Oh, it's you Ted,' her tone was flat; edged with disappointment. 'No, no,' she was saying, 'just felt like being on my own.' She listened, biting her bottom lip with discomfort before speaking again. 'Well yes, I guess it was rude leaving without thanking everyone, and yes, thank you for doing it for me.' After a brief pause and a slight change in tone she added, 'what ever would I do with out you.'

Ernest smiled to himself, thinking Ted's ego was too big to catch the intonation. Suddenly he heard a slight panic in Lisa voice.

'No Ted, please don't come around, I need to have some time alone.' After a brief pause listening to her caller she said, 'I promise I will not let Ernest tire me out with his talking.' In fact I was just about to go back home and change my clothes. Lisa made a face at Ernest and his eyebrows went up.

Then taken by complete surprise, Lisa was pulled back suddenly and held tightly against a broad chest smelling of a mixture of tobacco smoke and talcum powder.

Lisa stared at him for a moment, ready to defend herself against this show of male chauvinism, but the annoyance melted. The man standing there looking so innocent, was too much of a father figure to her.

Chapter 11

The doorbell rang. 'What the heck?' said Lisa as she sprang up to go to the front door. It was Jiten who had just arrived in a police car and was obviously reporting for duty. Lisa ushered her detective constable Smith into the front room to wait for her, while she continued to change into her working clothes.

Two red blotches appeared on Lisa's cheeks and her eyes lit up in anticipation. Then the annoying need for clearing her throat returned as she struggled to push her arms into the jacket Jiten was holding out for her.

Standing in the partially open doorway, D.C Smith experienced his emotions swinging between excitement and sympathy as he watched Lisa franticly rummaging through her pockets for her I.D, wallet and notebook. She lifted a hand in a salute and nearly missed the step.

'Oh hell.' she exclaimed falling against the detective constable's solid frame. He winced at her choice of words she invariably used and made for the car with Lisa pushing him forward to hurry. Just at that moment a small brown Ford Escort Focus was rounding the corner by the Horseshoe and coming straight for them, its indicator still flashing.

'Go.'

Lisa's shrill voice shouted from the police car's passenger side; in two seconds flat P.C. Smith was at the wheel and turning the key. The police car moved forward; spun around the triangle of the village green, turned the corner and was already entering the main road as Ted leapt out of his car.

Ted could only stand and stare at the empty road. Turning to look for the third figure he had seen outside he was now faced with a locked front door and a marmalade cat grinning at him through the window of number 7. Somewhat bewildered by the turn of events he had no choice but to go back to the farm, telling himself he would speak to Lisa later about her erratic behaviour.

Detective Constable Smith took a furtive look at his companion, Lisa sat stiff and stony-faced; her eyes fixed on the ribbon of road ahead. Smith pushed his foot down harder on the accelerator, and switched on the siren. This was his first homicide and he wanted to get there as quickly as possible, despite his mixed emotions.

It took only a few minutes to hit the roundabout which caused a slight panic among the other drivers as the cars already rounding it were left wondering where they had read about police cars with sirens screaming, coming up from behind them and whether they should to pull over to the right or carry on to the first exit. Another few minutes and the police car had passed through the town and whistled up the steep hill that overlooked it. At the top on the right stood the Saxon Arms.

A lone constable standing at the entrance, moved to stand in front of the approaching police car waving his arms. Lisa's window slid down and she flicked open her I.D at him.

The hotel drive was short and made of crushed stone. A sign indicated the parking ground; already half full with police vehicles and a forensic van. A group of people stood to one side, their discussions stopping briefly, stilled by the new arrivals, but then quickly resumed their focus and theories on what they had seen or heard.

A blue and white tape spanned the entrance of the hotel with yet another uniformed officer standing in front. Seeing it was the detective sergeant, he gave a quick salute and stepped back smartly, opening the glass doors to the reception area of the hotel.

Chief Superintendent Wigfull's solid figure moved quickly forward his hand outstretched with a look of pure relief on his face. He never quite gave the expression of commanding any situation; the tailored uniform never in keeping with the bulky frame it clung to. All this however belied the intellectual and serious mind that had taken quickly him up the ladder of his profession.

Grapping her hand, he shook it vigorously as a signal he understood what day it was and extending his sympathy; signalling to someone while still drawing her over to a private corner out of earshot.

Lisa followed; frowning at this delay in viewing the crime scene. The chief superintendent caught her restlessness. He signalled for two coffees for them both before speaking; his voice low and confidential.

'Bad news followed by good news I hope, which I'm afraid will all depend on you, Pharies.' He gave her a searching look; assessing her emotional state, but finding only a blank, but serious face.

'Our detective inspector is at this moment fighting for his life in the City Hospital.' He stated the information as if he was reading an e-mail. 'Seems like the man had a heart attack this morning.'

The news stunned Lisa. The man was not that much older than herself. People didn't have heart attacks until they were retired. She opened her mouth to say something, anything really, but nothing emerged. The chief hadn't finished yet, the worry lines all the time deepening on his forehead.

'No replacement as yet either; the bomb scare has us all wrapped up___; government priority.'

Lisa knew all about the explosives found in a house bordering on the Manchester area. It was a sensitive time just after the London IRA bombings: All police stations on top alert and information top priority.

'So who's heading up the homicide team sir?' she asked; her mind racing with names and faces. Someone handed her a coffee. She wrapped her hands around the polystyrene cup and blew on the hot liquid, raising her eyes at the same time for a response to her question. The response came in the form of another question; one that sent ripples of excitement through her. Did he really say what she thought she'd heard?

The chief superintendent looked uncomfortable and shifted his weight from one foot to the other. Much taller than Lisa, he bent forward slightly to catch her expression as a possible clue to her reply.

'Well,' he asked again a little concerned that he'd overstepped himself by intruding on her grief, but failed to understand a better way.

'Well, will you take over until someone comes available?'

The cup jerked and wavered in Lisa's hand, spilling some of the contents and scalding the flesh. It went unnoticed, her focus already on her new position. It never crossed her mind she couldn't take on the responsibility. All she'd ever aspired to was to be heading up her very own case.

She was made like her mentor Ernest, and thrived on investigating and coming up with the answer. She nodded.

'Good.' Her superior was already making to move away. 'Ah, here comes the good doctor.' He stopped and beckoned a small rotund figure over to them. 'All yours Pharies,' he said, before taking long strides to cross the wooden floor to the door.

The police surgeon's head was as round as his body. His merry personality made life a little less stressful when faced with a mutilated or badly burnt body. He was popular with the officers; his eyes twinkled in the puffy flesh above rosy cheeks.

'Hope you've already eaten.' He half joked; it was his way of telling her the murder victim was not a pretty sight, then remembering Lisa's circumstance looked half sheepish and waited for her to pull out her notebook and pencil.

He gave her information before she was able to ask her first question.

'Around 6 am, give or take an hour.' He never would comment to an exact time.

Lisa made a note of it; the pencil hovering for the next piece of information.

'Throat cut, right-handed, probably a carving knife by the depth.' he offered; looking around to trace the source of the smell of coffee.

Lisa wanted no distractions so she swooped in quickly.

'Age?'

'About my age.'

Lisa glared at him. She'd no idea how old the police surgeon was. There too much fat for wrinkles and he still had a fair head of sandy hair. He looked hurt but obliged.

'Forty-eight about___.' He emphasized "about", he was always cautious 'til facts were proven. 'Not a pretty sight,' he ventured; eyeing her up for any sign of an overactive stimulation, but seeing only a deadpan face and her controlled manner, he reckoned it was safe to proceed.

'In my opinion, whoever did it intended to. It was clean; no struggle, the carotid artery sliced deep and neatly judged by the amount of blood.'

'Yes, thank you Dr. Grimshaw for your thoughts, but the coroner will establish the facts now; you have analyzed death and time, that's all I need.' Her voice was icy, her gaze steady.

'So this is the way of things' mused the doctor. Each to their own job and kept in their place. Things had turned the corner and he didn't like it in the latter years of his career; no respect anymore.

Giving the acting detective inspector a lingering look, he excused himself. 'Let her find her own way to the murder scene,' he mused. He'd had enough.

She watched his figure move quickly, and suddenly realized she was standing alone in the reception room without a clue as to which corridor to take or the number of the room. Holding her head up high with all the confidence in the world for the benefit of any onlookers, she made for the corridor the doctor had emerged from. Thankfully halfway down the corridor, a constable was standing outside the room she wanted. She marched quickly along the narrow green and yellow hallway, the brown carpet sporting a faded scroll pattern. Judging by the constable's quizzical look, she realized she was about to step into a scene more resembling a slaughterhouse.

The victim's body was slumped awkwardly against the bed's headboard; the look on the face seemed surprised and fixed. A deep gapping slash opened the neck, the dark congealed blood already clotted and turned purple. Behind the once yellow rose pattered wallpaper, it looked as if a bottle of red ink had been thrown at it, striking with a force then trickling down like fondue. Her eyes traveled to the low ceiling tracing more trails of red. The doctor was right; it was no place for a weak stomach.

Lisa swallowed the bile down that rose up her oesophagus. It came as bit of a shock when she realized that the three people wearing white protective clothing, boots and masks were assessing her. Their status and the quiet methodical way they were going about their business screamed at her___. "Don't touch."

She acknowledged their concerns by nodding and placing her hands firmly in her pockets and watching them resume bagging items and dusting for fingerprints. A chalk mark was run along the headboard outlining the position of the victim's head. Lisa stepped out of the way, whilst a female dressed in the similar white garb took photographs from every angle.

Lisa studied every detail before directing her attention to the nearest forensic guy.

"Anything of interest in the case?" she asked pointing towards the open leather brief case. He shook his head; pulling down the mask and taking a deep breath.

'No papers if that's what you mean;' having assessed something was probably missing and the victim killed for it.

'Still mustn't make any prejudgments,' Lisa told herself. She didn't like it in others and tried to refrain from it herself, however much Ernest had told her to trust her first impressions.

'Who is he?' Forensics must have looked at his ID before bagging it and she wanted to be one up before asking the hotel manager.

'Thomas Reece, he is a professor from Oxford.'

'University?' Lisa asked. The forensic gave her a queer look.

Lisa left the room walking in the opposite direction along the corridor from the way she'd come. She was right, there was a door at the end and it opened onto the corner end of the drive, close to the edge of a wooded hill.

Turning back the way she'd come, her mind clicked into gear. First notify the victims relatives, find out why he was here in the hotel. Was he meeting some one? Any telephone calls? Her mind moved like lighting, all the time aware the first twenty-four hours of any homicide were crucial for gathering clues.

She was already on her mobile before she entered the reception hall and had organized statements from the manager down to the garbage man she'd seen out front.

All the guests were brought from their rooms as none had been allowed to leave and statements were taken.

Nothing significant came to the fore, apart from two phone calls relayed to the professor's room earlier that morning. A quick check found they were disappointingly from local phone boxes and the caller couldn't be identified.

Chapter 12

Jenny leaned her back against the rough cold stone of her cottage wall. She was outside at the back of the cottage, sitting on an old wooden three-legged stool; her dress was lifted high and one foot daggled over her knee.

She ran her hands over the wet surface of her leg, feeling the softness of the dew droplets that glistened on the skin. Her other foot, resting on a cold flagstone still harboured grass seeds and damp grass from the fields.

A piece of old towelling lay limply over her thighs ready to dry the morning dew from her legs. It would be an automatic gesture and done too many times to count; her mind remaining with the feeling of the fresh earth. It was still too early for anyone to be about, although at one time there were night workers at the mill and she had to walk further afield to keep out of sight of prying eyes.

The changes from night to day were supple. The dawn starting with a soft lightness of the sky that changed second by second, almost at the blink of an eye, to pastel colours of pink and yellow before merging into a painting of deep reds, oranges and finally blue and generally followed by the dawn chorus; the many birdcalls bringing their own magical sounds to her world. Only those who were truly awake could witness this transformation. Unfortunately most workers arriving at the mill were generally too busy or too late to get lost in this passing beauty of nature. Once the mill engines started, the daily sound of the workers cars would break these moments of tranquillity and things would not be the same until the evening.

This particular morning the horizon was rippled with many hues, even the first rays of the early sun could be felt. No clouds gathered as they usually did at this time of the year, the sky promising a nice day. A kingfisher called from the rushes by the river's bank and was answered by its mate.

The foliage of the trees from the wood across the field trembled with the restless flapping of wings in their branches. The soft rustle of grass as the rabbits ran along familiar paths and the occasionally shriek of a badger calling its young and always the ever present rhythmic melody of the river.

So it was that Jenny's spirit renewed itself daily with the stirring of life on the land around her. From the time she'd held her mother's hand as a child and walked happily barefoot to feel the fresh dew on the ground, it had been a spiritual experience that had never left her.

This land was the one she clung to with every fibre of her body. This was Simkins' land, each creature her family; the river the very blood in her arteries. Without it nothing would be the same. She once thought her heart would stop like the giant wheel race of the old mill had, if she couldn't be there. That was before Peter was born and now she knew without doubt it would always be their land as long as one of them lived on it.

For Peter it would be different; the land would become different too, as it had been over the centuries. But she had taught him to love it, not the way she had been taught at school, but by the knowledge of its true value.

She'd never taught him the healing plants of nature, although had often used them for his childhood ailments and he had not questioned those bunches of hanging herbs in the kitchen or their intended use. He just accepted her ways as being the old country ways.

No, this wasn't to be her son's life. She had other plans for him. Everything rested on Peter.

She thought of Hugo and found it difficult to ease the waves of anxiety or the fast beating of her heart after his visit. The letter she'd received from Oxford had greatly unsettled her. Things were happening too fast, but on reflection Hugo posed a threat that called for a supple solution.

A sweet smell of lavender floated in the air. Jenny lifted her head. She felt her mother's presence, a sudden the ache for her guidance. The feeling was stronger than usual. All her inner senses became finely tuned, sometimes she thought of it as a silver thread that connected daughter to mother, then right down to the one that spoke to them of the land.

Suddenly she laid the towel aside, got up and entered the cottage. First she listened, her attention trained on Peter's small room upstairs. Silence. All was quiet, She glanced at the clock; it was earlier than she thought.

Jenny walked over to the small but solid Welsh dresser and began to empty the cupboards and drawers. It was much too heavy to move with everything in it.

When it was eventually empty she stood to one side of it and tried to pull it away from the wall. It wouldn't budge.

Panic began to arise within her. She'd never considered she wouldn't be able to move the dresser. Only once had she witnessed her mother doing it, but Jenny's frame was not as robust and strong.

She took a deep breath and pulled with all her might. This time it moved little. Then, inching it over the tile flooring bit by bit, it edged out a little further each time before sliding easily over the floor's remaining hard but worn surface.

Jenny sighed with relief.

Holding her breath to suck in her stomach she slid half her body behind the dresser feeling for the crevice in the wall. She sighed as she found what she was groping for. Carefully she edged out the box pushed into a hole in the wall and slid it towards her.

Walking over to the bottom of the stairs she listened again; . . . . silence.

She laid the ancient box on the table and drew up a chair, spending a few moments just looking at it. The box was old, so old that the wood had blackened yet the silver hinges retained their shape, although black too with wont of polish to show off their worth. There was a keyhole, but it was not locked.

Jenny lifted the lid and gently pulled out the cracked dried parchment, laying it flat before her. As a child she hadn't quite understood when her mother had shown it to her and had explained its message, as she couldn't read then. Even now she had trouble reading it, all the S's looking like F's.

She glanced again at the clock and hastily rolled the parchment up. Running her finger around the inside of the box, she found what she'd reached in it for. Jenny pulled out a round object and slipped it into her pocket. The box was closed hurriedly, pushed back into the cavity and with renewed energy; Jenny pushed the dresser back into place. This time it slid back easier.

Hearing a noise she turned with a start. Peter stood watching her; rubbing his eyes.

'What are you doing?' he asked sleepily. 'I heard a noise.'

Jenny's breathing was still fast after the exertion, but didn't betray her shock at seeing her son. She walked over to him and patted his rear as she turned him around to face the stairs.

'Off you go love, back to bed.' Jenny's voice was controlled and gentle. 'I'm starting a little spring cleaning early that's all.'

Peter took one look at the dresser's contents piled around, accepted the explanation and returned to the warmth of his bed. Jenny sat down. She felt a little sick and a wave of anxiety hit her again.

'John's Wort. That's what is needed,' she murmured; searching the hanging herbs drying on a ceiling rack, all the time her finger curled around the article in her pocket. Bringing it to light, she laid it on the table and sat looking at it. The solid silver ring still had lustre and colour, but it was the stone that held her gaze.

It was oval, the colour of amber, with a whitish shape within the stone. Small flecks of bright orange caught the light as she picked it up and ran her fingers over its smoothness.

She placed it on her middle finger, instinctively knowing it would fit. Then holding up her hand she gazed fascinated at the toadstone in its silver setting.

'Four hundred years,' she whispered to herself. She rubbed it again, her voice a little louder, although still barely audible. 'I need all your energy now, and will not take it off till all is finished.'

A shaft of early morning light broke through the window, catching the flecks in the amber, and playing with the specks of colour.

'All is well,' Jenny uttered out loud this time, as a new confidence arose inside her; the John's Wort forgotten.

Then out of the blue, she was aware of something wrong; a sound, a presence. She couldn't place her finger on it. The back door was slightly ajar, and she couldn't remember whether she'd closed it. She stepped outside. The gate was off its latch and Jenny was certain she'd closed it. Looking over towards the mill she now saw John's car parked.

A frown came over her face as she turned thoughtfully indoors.

Chapter 13

Kristen was bent over the accounts books that John had brought home. She knew they were not meant for her or Hugo's eyes by the way they had been hidden between magazines in the locked briefcase. Fortunately for her and unfortunately for John, he'd left the small brass key in his jacket pocket.

Kristen had at that time been more interested in handkerchiefs with marks of lipstick or notes with hurried phone numbers written on them. The briefcase keys an added bonus to her power over her handsome but weak husband.

Once she would have laughed at the position of strength it gave her, having never kidded herself it lay in her looks. Kristen had the gift of seeing things just how they were and had never once deluded herself into thinking that John found her irresistible. She only had to look in the mirror to know there was no real beauty in the face that looked back at her.

Her power and only power to get what she wanted was money, and there had always been plenty of that she had always presumed.

It came as a nasty shock as she looked over the account books and saw bills owed, and interest charges building up. Frowning, her trained eye flew down the columns of figures quickly knowing that she had signed the cheques to cover all costs.

Then it hit her, she felt sick. She'd signed all right, but only blank cheques. John always filled them in. Her initial reaction was one of anger at what her husband had been doing, before turning on herself for being such a fool. How many times had Dr. Potts said John may have a lot to offer in one department, but was quite dim in others. She had laughed at the doctor, saying; 'that was just the way she liked it.'

Dr Potts had been wrong on the first account though, John's efforts had never produced anything, and now she was past hoping for the chance of producing a child.

Biting the pencil between her teeth that she held lengthways in her mouth, helped release the tension. She watched tiny flakes of yellow paint flake off and fluttering onto the paper.

Pushing the rotating chair around the floor on its wheels, she leaned back and turned facing the portrait of her father hanging over the marble mantelpiece.

It wasn't the best of oil paintings, but showed a great likeness to him. It had been commissioned when her grandfather had died and her father inherited the land and mill.

His small dark eyes appeared like a couple of blackcurrants in a pasty white face.

Straight eyebrows. They would have been nice on a female, but most odd looking on the male of the species. The nose was long and thin until the end where it flared out, showing little of the insides of the nostrils.

Kristen ran her finger down the bridge of her own nose, recognizing the gene for that particular organ she'd inherited. Her eyes too were like his, round and piecing. Only the mouth differed. His was full and sensual, whilst she had her mother's; small and thin that needed lipstick to give it shape and fullness.

Kristen stared at her father's face, contemplating the distinct resemblance of kinship. Then her mind slid to Hugo, with his fair thick hair, grey eyes and handsome features, before reflecting on the mother who died giving him birth.

She was ten at the time; remembering that dreadful night well; the pale figure lying on the sheets, that still had blood stains seeping through them. The new baby wrinkled and swaddled in a blue blanket sheet crying powerfully in the crib; her father's figure bending over it with such a look of satisfaction.

He'd taken little notice of his daughter, the silent dark-haired girl staring at the cold statue on the large bed, whose fair hair lay limp against its marble skin, and the grey eyes unseeing. His lack of attention didn't bother her; at least she'd always thought it didn't. She had grown up knowing that the Ravencroft males were more important; adding to the line of land ownership, unbroken for centuries. The very name Ravenscroft was all that mattered. All at once she wanted to laugh, to stand in front of the cold Ravenscroft and laugh loudly saying,

'What now father? Will your precious son do his duty? He certainly hasn't shown much interest as yet, and it seems your daughter was given the brains not your son;' her voice tinged with bitterness.

She got up and stood beneath the flat canvas looking up. Her father's small beady eyes held a frosty glare. The artist had captured them well, the long thin nose flaring at the nostrils, and a thin self-righteous mouth holding in his contempt for others.

His straight black hair was untouched by grey as it highlighted the whiteness of the then fashionable starch collar carefully aligned with a thin plain tie.

Kristen's eyes travelled to the tiepin. It was now Hugo's, but never worn. It had a solid gold letter R with a long tail.

She thought of her brother's fair hair, good looks and grey eyes; their mother's softer features had passed onto him. It was uncanny how two offsprings from the same parents could turn out so different. When she was younger she would have traded willingly, but not now. The hurt she'd once felt at not being acknowledged as important as her brother had lessened, when Hugo made her his partner in the mill. Not that he had much alternative, as she had always been the smarter of the two.

She frowned, now fully aware of her only weakness. She should never have let John become the manager. She looked over to the account sheets and frowned; absentmindedly stroking her chin, as she thought of her practicality; so free of emotion.

No one, not even John was going to lose one penny of the mill's capital. The land was to be theirs for centuries to come. Hugo would marry and have children and the Ravenscroft line would go on. Of these facts; she was determined.

Some ten miles away John was unaware of the storm that was brewing. He had left the mill just before lunch, changed his clothes at home and now was heading for the Black Boar.

The British racing green Spitfire cruised along the road gathering envious glances from the local youths who held dreams of owing one some day.

John slowed down. The Black Boar stood at the junction where the road divided one going to Manchester and the other to Macclesfield.

The sixteenth century building had been declared as a heritage site and had put a stop to any ambitious road improvement plans.

Slipping easily between two larger cars on the car park, John gathered an attaché case from the seat beside him and lifted his long legs out. He never thought of closing the canvas top to prevent someone stealing it. It was too unusual a car not to be recognised on its journey to some dingy garage.

He felt a little high, like the days he'd experimented with an occasional weed. Although never pursued it to the point of addiction. Neither was he a heavy drinker, a glass of cream sherry sipped at leisure his only form of alcoholic intake.

However his journey to the Black Boar was not for want of a pick-me-up, but a good lunch and a very profitable meeting: the second taking preference. He glanced at his Rolex, a habit he found himself doing sometimes just for the shear pleasure of seeing it on his wrist. Today the time was more important, ten to one.

Early and that's just the way he liked it when any negotiations were imminent. John liked to choose his position at the table and always liked to face the door. Every since he'd seen the film The Godfather in his youth, he'd been impressed by the power it gave the person facing the arrivals as they walked towards him.

Today was no different, although it was only one person he would be watching walk over to him. The table had to be small and private. John pushed the swing doors forward as he walked through into the snug. The hinges creaked till the momentum of the doors lessened and finally came to rest.

Right away John knew where he wanted to sit. It was a quiet corner, a window would be to his rear giving light to his companion's face, and giving him accommodation on the bench seat for his attaché case.

He'd hardly sat down when he was aware of a spotty faced waitress hovering over him with a pencil already paused over a notebook. 'Do you want to order?'

His solar plexus was pumping out adrenaline. 'Sherry.' he managed to utter. For some reason his space and plans seemed unhinged by the waitress's aggressive manner. He pulled himself together quickly and gave her a charming smile.

'I'm waiting for a friend dear, give us a minute or two before we order a meal.' It worked like it always did, she grinned back showing her uneven teeth.

'Right you are luv,' she said, striding over to an elderly couple, who had abandoned their cutlery and were pushing long thick chips, dipped in tomato sauce into their mouths.

The clock over the blackened stone mantel surround showed exactly one o'clock, John's gaze travelled to the swing doors. Bang on time, his quarry was walking straight for him, giving a quick nod of the head and claiming the opposite chair.

Their eyes locked for a moment, and John was the first to look away. He took a deep breath to steady the quivering muscles of his hands.

'Drink?' he asked the new comer; signalling to the waitress, who had decided to take her time coming over and finished wiping a table with renewed vigour. 'It's on me,' added John, a little put off by the lack of enthusiasm.

'Suit yourself.' John retorted soberly and ordered another sherry. He lifted the lid of the brief case beside him and tapped it. 'Nothing under five grand, you understand.' The man opposite to him nodded his agreement.

John, taking a sip of the sherry and peering over his glass, had hoped to see some emotion that would give him power, but the eyes looking back at him were full of contempt. He fought for control. Funny, although a deal was struck; he felt he hadn't actually won. It was disconcerting. He downed the sherry in one; something he'd never done in his life. It made him slightly dizzy, but armoured him against the panic attack awaiting its onset.

'Cash?' his visitor questioned.

'Yes, but not new notes mind.' John felt his speech a little slurred, but was beginning to feel back in control. He was too clever to wind up in a mess. This would be a Godsend and would straighten out all his problems.

The deal was done. With arrangements made to John's satisfaction; he let his companion sneak a look at the contents of his case. He felt a little disappointed there was no lunching together and maybe more talk on the matter just for interest's sake, but it wasn't to be. He found himself alone and feeling rather hungry.

He hailed the waiter again and ordered a full blown lunch.

Chapter 14

By the evening Lisa was shattered. No one had seen anything unusual; nobody had asked the hotel staff which room the murdered man was in. In fact the hours of interviewing had come up negative of any leads; no matter how insignificant.

The victim's name had been established as Professor Thomas Reece from Oxford, the information in his wallet corresponded with his name from the booking of the room.

'No one had asked about him,' said the worried looking manager knowing only too well that all this wasn't going to do the hotel any good, at least for a while, although he harboured a sneaking idea that the curious might fill the dining rooms and bar. Still it was the rooms that brought in the money and no one wanted to be in a room with a murderer at large, so in the final analysis there seemed no gain.

One shaken room maid said she'd seen a man enter room 302 late at night, but after a lot of probing the woman who had booked the room admitted it was her male friend, and did they really need to tell her husband? Lisa wrote down the details and thought it would serve her right if the husband was in on the interviews anyway. However seeing the panic on the woman's face, Lisa affirmed that if she was telling the truth and it could be collaborated, there was no need to implicate her male visitor. Ernest had been very good at calming people's fears of police involvement. Knowing this was a fine line however; she wasn't about to compromise herself.

There had been a couple of phone calls to the murder room, but both from pay-phone boxes. Still at least she now knew the professor had contacts in the town who knew where he was, and anyone of them could have visited him.

The next job would be to contact Oxford and find his nearest relative or whoever knew him well. This needed to be arranged quickly. Leaving these instructions to the staff completing the remaining forensic examination, Lisa beckoned to her detective constable and they made for the car.

The police headquarters were as busy as any beehive. Tables had been set up in Incident Room in front of a white paper flip chart. Coffee was percolating and cookies had been sent for as the team grouped excitedly. The news that the detective inspector was in hospital had circulated quickly; all eyes now turned to his replacement in the form of acting Detective Inspector Pharies. There were a number of sympathetic glances from among the group; those remembering she had been called in from her mother's funeral that very day.

Lisa felt the atmosphere but packed her inner emotions away. Shifting some tables forward, she stood behind instead of in front of them, and glanced through some folders.

The other departments had not let her down. She motioned to Detective Constable Smith to pick up the ink marker and write on the flipchart, and then continued in a clear loud voice,

'Name . . . Thomas Reece.'

Step by step, all the information was written down clearly on each flip-chart page; to be removed when full and placed around the room for everyone to see. The Oxford police had informed them that the professor lived alone; no known relatives, very few acquaintances and all living within the confines of the university. His PhD. was in medieval history of which he indulged himself totally, according to all that knew him. Never married; his next of kin a cousin in Canada who had been informed but was too old and ill to travel.

'So,' said Lisa; looking at her notes. 'It seems the professor came to see some person or persons in or near this town. We know he had a briefcase with him, but whatever was in it was removed and taken. It suggests that the contents may have been the reason he was killed.'

She stood silent for a moment. A thought had occurred to her, as the crime scene came back to her. 'And the person who took them came with the intention of leaving no evidence of his identity.' She looked at the concerned sea of faces around her. Only the burping of the coffee percolator could be heard. 'Whoever it was, brought along the murder weapon.' Again Lisa stopped before adding; 'why bring along a knife if it wasn't intended for use?'

Someone in the room added, 'Whatever was in the brief case was extremely important,'

'Blackmail?' queried another.

At this suggestion, the room quickly filled with the buzzing of voices, then tapered off to quietness again as a door opened and the police photographer pushed his way to the front of the room. Pulling out a couple of prints from a large brown envelope; he handed them to Lisa. He smiled at Lisa. Moving his hand across his throat; he indicated the cause of death, and then left.

Lisa pinned them up. It wasn't a pretty sight, and no matter how hardened one was and how many battered bodies had been dealt with in the past, it was always a shock that this human being was no more than an animal in a slaughterhouse.

The body of a middle-aged man was slumped by the bed; a gaping slash in the neck, eyes were wide open with a hint of surprise and all around the splashes of blood. Lisa waited a minute for it all to sink in before continuing.

'We have a sadistic killer on our hands that planned this in great detail. Most likely male from the extent of the violence displayed; knew the hotel layout as he most certainly entered and left by a side door without being seen, suggesting whoever it was knew the layout of the hotel rooms.'

'Could it be a person working at the hotel?' Someone in the room asked.

Lisa considered the question carefully before answering: 'A possibility yes, but the telephone call received gives us a clue to the fact that it was someone he'd made contact with and possible knew, so right now I want to map out where the telephone booths are in the town, especially those near to the hotel. Talk to people around these places. I want to learn more about the professor from the people who knew him; maybe had a full picture of the guy, even to his sexual preferences.'

There was a giggle, which quickly trailed off suddenly into a cough as the owner caught sight of Lisa's steely gaze.

'Someone, somewhere wanted something he had with him and that is probably the reason for his murder. Let's consider blackmail, something valuable, but also remember the Prof was passionate about history. What had he got that someone would kill for and why would he travel here? 'Was he meeting with someone from our town?'

She stopped for a moment considering her own evaluation before making a decision. 'I want to know of any group around here that deals with ancestry.'

All at once the little energy she had seemed to run out and she clutched the table for support to stop her swaying. A clap was heard, and then another, until the whole room was applauding the woman who had just lost her mother, but was now more than ready to lead her team. Lisa felt slightly dizzy. She knew she needed to rest, just a few hours of oblivion and she would be ready to go again.

Someone brought her a much-needed coffee. It tasted metallic and reminded her of eating pudding from a silver spoon that had just been cleaned with cleaning paste. She put the metal beaker down, promising herself one in a paper cup from the doughnut shop around the corner. The very thought of a jam filled doughnut reminded her that she hadn't eaten apart from the tiny funeral sandwiches earlier. Maybe in that case, perhaps having two donuts would be okay. Oh what the hell; a chocolate éclair as well. There was no way she intended to cook tonight.

She pushed past her colleagues with a fixed smile on her face, nodding to their show of consideration for her well being; emotionally that was. Mentally they knew she could out strip them all when focused.

Donuts it was then; the detective constable selecting a bagel for himself, before driving her home. D.C. Smith had heard her loud and clear, when she remarked she didn't want to be disturbed for the rest of the evening.

Dropping her off and waiting until the key was in the door, the detective constable drove slowly past the Horseshoe and took the Belton road back. A speeding brown Ford Escort passed him, hugging the middle of the road and nearly sending him into the ditch.

P.C. Smith chased after the offending car and flagged him down. He was going to enjoy this.

Chapter 15

Lisa gave the driver of the police car a short wave after he'd waited for her to find the key to her home. But she never opened the front door, for as soon as her detective constable was out of sight she hurried around to number 11.

She'd hardly had time to press the bell button when the door opened wide. Ernest stood aside to let her pass. He waited in silence whilst his visitor pulled off her coat and dumped it across the small chair used in the hall to sit on while fixing shoelaces. Coat removed; shoes kicked off with a flick of her toes to each heel.

Lisa up to this point hadn't said a word. Ernest kept his patience as if uninterested in her behaviour and pushed open the parlour door to let her pass. The fire was still lit, as was the table lamp, the shadows of evening were creeping in slowly. On the small coffee table was a bottle of Pinot Noir and two glasses.

Lisa flopped down, her eyes never leaving Ernest's face as he filled the two glasses. She took a sip letting it lubricate the back of her throat, its passage feeling restricted. There was too much interrupting any possible verbalization. Her whole body was switched on to full throttle, yet one push and it would just burn out. Exhausted; her need to relax and sleep was hovering over her like the wings of some giant bird.

It was Ernest who broke the silence, bringing some normality to the prevailing situation. 'Rita was able to catch a flight to London and will be home tonight.' He waited, and finding little response continued, 'in fact I'm picking her up later tonight. The train arrives at Crewe in two hours.'

This time Lisa nodded, she felt a warm safe feeling passing through her muscles relaxing the excitement and tension of the day. Finishing off the wine she offered her empty glass to be filled again and took a long deep breath.

Watching the face in front of her for any reaction, she stated. 'It's my case now Gov.; the homicides are all mine.'

At first Ernest frowned with puzzlement, and then his facial creases cleared as he recalled the nation's priorities. He knew every experienced officer in the force was needed and he'd always known it was only a matter of time before Lisa's name would come up for promotion. He grinned, his reply hanging tantalizingly in the air between them.

'So now we are equals lass. Well done.' He leaned across, patting her knee with affection and fatherly pride, as if Lisa had been his own daughter.

'Detective Inspector Pharies,' he murmured, watching the blood rise to her cheeks. 'Well, well.'

Lisa moved a little with some discomfort; maybe, she'd not yet informed him that she was only an "acting" inspector, but then she knew only too well that would be the next step for her, that is if she did a good job in clearing up this homicide quickly and efficiently.

Her hand shook a little. She steadied it but not before the red wine went into oscillation and some spilled. Her mind was racing again; too many details spinning together, no answers to any of her questions as yet. The waiting for forensics and the medical examiner all took time.

Suddenly and without any warning she unloaded on her old boss. She wanted his guidance, experience, and his uncanny intuition that brought results.

Ernest listened, his inner vision relating to the usual processes involved during any homicide. So intent was Lisa on using Ernest as a check for all the areas needed to be covered off, that when he coolly asked who the victim was, she blurted it out, 'A professor, Thomas Reece.'

She stopped horrified at herself. She'd already committed a no-no, knowing that the victim's name was always withheld until relatives had been informed. She felt sick as she prepared herself for her mentor's look of disappointment.

It didn't appear. Instead a look of surprise and a hint of sorrow passed over Ernest's face like a veil; leaving a questioning expression that suddenly seemed momentarily personal.

'Go on,' urged Ernest. He was not looking at her but gazing at the ceiling.

'Hell Ernest, I've already failed in the job by revealing the victim's identity to you so soon.' He turned towards her with a blank look as Lisa continued, 'I told you who he was before informing those who knew him.' Even that hadn't come out right, as she'd meant to say "before the next of kin had been informed."

'But I knew him,' said Ernest. The words stated succinctly and very clearly.

'What?' she said, as she jerked back in confusion.

'I knew him.' Ernest repeated and went on to describe the man on the train journey. 'He got off at Crewe with me; I saw him hail a taxi. He raised a hand at her, indicating this information was for her to follow up on.

Lisa remembered all too clearly, as she recalled. 'Yes, the arrival time of the train and his subsequent movements can be checked against the time he booked in at the Saxon Hotel.'

Lisa shook her head. 'He must have gone straight to the hotel, but I'll check the taxis anyway.' She looked thoughtful. 'Someone or some others knew he was arriving and where he was staying at the Saxon.' She stopped his next question by telling him there were some local calls from a phone box.

Ernest sighed, 'Well, at least someone knew of him in the town.'

Lisa frowned. 'So what did you and he talk about? Did he mention why he was coming here in the first place?'

'Talk about?' The question was directed at the white ceiling, the owner of the voice detaching itself into contemplation. 'He told me he was a professor of medieval history at Oxford. I assumed he meant the university.'

'Hmm,' Lisa's tone indicating this fact was already known.

'Let me think,' there was a lengthy pause followed by a slap as his hand hit the arm of his chair. 'He said we were alike, he and I; I solved crimes of today and he solved crimes committed in the past.'

'What did he mean by that?' questioned Lisa; focusing her attention on every word offered.

'Witchcraft.'

'What?'

'Witchcraft.' Ernest's eyes fell and stared at her. 'He talked of witchcraft and tales about witches.'

Lisa's mouth dropped, she didn't comprehend any of Ernest's ramblings, she glanced at the wine bottle, and there was still some wine left, a pity to leave it. Suddenly her attention snapped back to the speaker in front of her.

'His ring,' said Ernest, 'now what the dickens did he call it?'

Lisa could only sit and wait for some explanation, but was well versed in her old gov.'s insignificances. He'd already focused in on something she'd missed.

'What ring?' she almost yelled, 'He wasn't wearing a bloody ring.'

Ernest mouth opened slightly, his eyes retreated under the brows, and two hard lines folded in a groove between them.

'His ring Lisa,' he lifted his hand staring at it, remembering the other's hand. 'He let me look at it. It was so unusual and I was fascinated.'

'His ring?' Lisa stated again. 'What was it like? . . . this ring.'

'A big broad ornate silver band holding an amber-coloured stone flecked inside.' He called it "a toadstone"; saying it was a talisman against witchcraft.'

Lisa frowned. 'Who would have wanted to take that?' She thought some more. 'Did he say why he'd come to this part of the country?'

'No. I just assumed it was some research he was undertaking,'

'Ernest,' Lisa's mind was now clicking trying to piece together things she had witnessed. 'He had a brief case.' Ernest looked interested. 'It was empty apart from a pen and a glasses case. The glasses were on the floor all bloodstained. He must have been wearing them.'

'And reading something,' added her confidant. 'Possibly something taken from the briefcase.'

They looked at each other; Ernest reached for the half filled bottle and filled the offered glass and his own. They both drank in silence.

'What had he got that was worth killing for?' He broke the quiet; speaking more to himself than Lisa, 'and why was the ring taken?'

'Do you think we are dealing with devil worship here, or that there is some group that practice it in this town?' Lisa took a gulp of her wine, almost choking as her words spilled out with a large amount of unease.

Ernest shrugged his shoulders. Stranger things had happened to him during his career, but he would be the first to admit never witchcraft.

The doorbell rang. Startled; they both looked at each other before looking at the clock.

'Oh hell.' Ernest got up quickly and tipped over the table sending the wine bottle spinning off it and landing by the hearth: A pool of red spread over the tiles.

A creaking sound; followed by a door closing and footsteps. Ernest's face was turning a funny colour, as Lisa caught on to his reaction. She wanted to giggle, but it didn't seem right.

'Poor Rita,' she mused. She must have been waiting at the train station, whilst they were drinking wine and involved in sorting out details of a crime scene. Instinct told Lisa not to stay around.

The room door opened and Rita had to slide to one side, to allow Lisa to pass, but Rita's eyes were already trained on the desperate look that her newly wedded husband was giving her.

Chapter 16

Jenny Simkins wrapped her hand-knitted shawl around her shoulders and shivered. The mornings were becoming chilly. Hugging the shawl closer to her chest, she bent over and gave the dying embers in the fireplace a poke. Placing a dry log on the top of them, the flames leapt like dancers twisting and turning.

Jenny moved the old rocking chair closer to the warmth before sitting in it and began gently rocking back and fro. She liked the early morning, the energy around her quiet and Peter safe in bed.

Last night had been different, sleep failed to come as she tossed and turned with images she couldn't get rid of. Quiet now, apart from the occasional creak in the rafters, tiredness overcame her.

Outside Jack Frost had laid a white carpet of hoar-frost turning the grass and plants into glassy sculptures of icy fantasies of nature. His handiwork glazed the windows in patterns envied by artists. Only the river continued on its century's old path past the mill and its unused but still slowly turning wheel-race.

Jenny stirred; unfolding her arms she laid her hand on her knee. Sleepy eyes caught the light of the fire in the ring she wore. She stared hypnotized at the moving patterns of light on the toadstone in the ring. Then suddenly she found herself being transported back down through the centuries. For a second Jenny was convinced the hand that held the ring was another's, not hers for the fingers were long and tapered, the skin white and unblemished, in contrast to her short fingers and rough skin.

Her lids closed. She was standing in the field by the river, but as she turned she saw a large grey stone house in the distance. Then out of nowhere came a woman walking towards her, holding the hand of a small boy.

Jenny's heart beat faster as she realized the child was Peter, dressed differently and with longer hair, but nevertheless was Peter.

A loud crack at the window broke the dream, and Jenny shot up in her chair. A few feathers mingled with blood smeared the frosty window.

Jenny sighed, her dream forgotten. She got up and padded across the stone flagged floor to the door. When opened a rush of cold air rushed in, but Jenny braved the cold and found what she had expected. A large black crow had crashed into the window. It happened occasionally, as birds see through it to the window on the other side of the room and the fields beyond. Normally she kept a curtain closed to stop this happening. Full of remorse Jenny picked up the lifeless carcass by the feet and threw it over the wall into the field, where nature would take care of it.

She went back inside, fragments of her dream still lingering in her mind. Sometimes she wondered which world she was truly living in. Her mother told her everything was interwoven, energy constantly changing. However sometimes it got locked in its own darkness, gathering strength to release itself at the right moment in time, like some gigantic volcano. She had hinted the Simkins' line was like that, and the time was near when its force would explode.

Jenny shivered not from cold but from apprehension; the signs could not be dismissed. She must be vigilant and above all cautious. Peter was all that mattered.

A few hours later the sun arose in the east like a giant orange globe, melting the delicate tracery and giving rise to rivulets of water that dripped off the grass and windows.

Slowly the world around Jenny stirred bringing the sounds so familiar; first the birds and forest creatures, then the purr of the cars as they entered the parking lots of the town's malls. Peter left for school and Jenny resumed her daily routine.

At the mill nobody noticed their manager was not around, as more times than not, he worked his own hours. Somebody did mention his car was parked outside and it was assumed the working day was the same as it had always been. Two things happened however to break the normal routine of the working day at the mill.

One of the workers had gone around the back of the mill for a smoke and found himself staring at a mangled body on the old mill wheel. At the same time the floor supervisor had gone into John's office and discovered blood splattered on the floor and walls.

By the time acting Detective Inspector Pharies arrived with her Detective Sergeant Smith, the whole of the work force was out trying to take their turn in viewing the body. The path around the back of the mill was narrow and only allowed room for one person at a time.

Straight away Lisa ordered Jitan to move the curious workers away, and patiently awaited re-enforcements and for 'Scene of Crime Officers' (SOCO). Nothing could be touched until the police photographer was satisfied with his pictures of the victim; now jammed on the stalled wheel race itself.

Within half an hour an hour, sirens still blasted out as more police cars arrived. After the necessary photos were taken, the body was removed which in itself proved dangerous. A sigh of relief went up when it was finally accomplished.

The police doctor had been called to the scene to give a rough estimate of the time of death, made all the more difficult by the constant flow of water over parts of the victims partially dismembered remains, while leaving other crime officers around to get on with their specific tasks.

Acting Detective Inspector Pharies stood back and waited patiently, all the time watching and looking around, taking in the whole scene and engraving it on her memory. Glancing up at the side of the old mill, she noted an open window above; slightly upstream of the mill wheel itself.

The doctor pushed his way towards her, his glasses wobbling dangerously on the end of his red nose. 'Can't be certain, but I'd say he died somewhere between nine and eleven last evening' he offered, as Lisa raised her eyes questioningly.

'No need to tell me how he died.' she said, as she gazed up at the window.

'Not so'. The doctor gave a chuckle as if he had come out a winner, and awaited the look of surprise on Lisa's face. 'Killed by a bullet,' he announced proudly as if he had scored a top mark. 'Right here,' he said, pointing to his neck.

'You mean he was shot and pushed through that window.' exclaimed Lisa looking up again.

'Yes, got it in one.' The doctor chuckled at the look of surprise on the acting detective inspector's face.

The body had now been lifted off the mill wheel, which was no minor task and the area around taped off as the special services team went about their thorough search.

Lisa watched as the body was bagged and zipped up, before making her way around the mill and through its doors.

Once inside, she made her way up to the two flights of stairs, noting that no elevators had ever been installed.

The office door was guarded by a young fresh faced constable who stepped aside smartly when she produced her identification. Once inside Lisa realised the SOCO team had been and gone, leaving outlines around the blood splashes and a bullet hole, that indicated one of the bullets must have missed the victim.

The window was still open and taped. Lisa walked cautiously across the floor and peered out of the window, her hands clasped lightly behind her back, just in case she was tempted to touch anything.

'Hell of a way to go'; the voice seemed to come out of no-where.

Lisa spun around coming to face-to-face with a man she'd never set her eyes on before. About her own age, he was tall thin and had the most blue eyes that Lisa had ever seen.

She stared at him for a moment, partly in confusion and partly out of curiosity, before gaining command of her voice. 'Who the hell are . . . .' she stopped as he lifted his hand.

'Tony Aubrey, criminal profiler,' he stated, watching the reaction on Lisa's face.

'What the hell . . . . '; her words coming out slowly and edged with disbelief.

Tony smiled, and for a moment Lisa bathed in its warmth; then just as quickly she brought herself to the present issue.

'What are you trying to tell me with your fancy psychology?' She'd blurted it out before she had time to think; having little patience with the new methods now being used to understand criminal behaviour.

Tony grinned, 'I'm here to find out what the murderer's mind is like and to try to help you.' His voice soft and controlled, as if he was used to the scepticism.

Lisa swallowed to lessen the cough that threatened to erupt. She leaned back against the window then quickly moved as she realised what she was doing. Tony watched and smiled, sensing her discomfort. 'The killer not only killed his victim but considered him rubbish too; hence the throwing away of the body through the window.'

'What on earth makes you come up with an idea like that?' said Lisa giving a little laugh that was almost a slight sneer.

Tony eyed her thoughtfully, he saw a strong intelligent woman, though vulnerable and slightly unsure of herself. Her need was to be in control.

Lisa's mind travelled its own path and was toying with the idea that the killer thought the river would carry the victim down stream, but then what good would that do, as it was clear the murder took place in this very room.

Lisa reddened and turned away, her mind now wondering if drugs were involved. When she turned, the profiler had gone and for a moment she felt cheated.

Jiten came through the door and saw her standing perplexed in the middle of the room.

'Alright gov?' he said with concern.

Lisa raised her head and looked at Jiten's open face, making her feel adjusted and in control again.

'Just thinking, make a note for me to inquire whether there were any drugs associated with the last victim and this.'

P.C Smith looked at her inquiringly, but Lisa wasn't ready yet to confess the profiler may have had a point. She muttered to herself; 'he'd said rubbish needs to be trashed,' but then she added; 'sounds more like drugs to me.'

Lisa left, closing the door behind her.

Chapter 17

Jenny stood in the doorway of her cottage, her ears trained on the police sirens and the blaring noise of an ambulance. The sounds were coming nearer and nearer, shattering the silence. Silence because the normal hum from the mill had ceased earlier; which happened from time to time, but never lasted this long. Something was very wrong and Jenny knew it.

Her view of the mill front was restricted by the square stone building that had once served as a washhouse and toilet. Now the large copper bowl held herbs and the shelves and racks used for drying plants and holding storage jars. The toilet fed a sceptic tank and was still in use.

Jenny stepped outside, wrapping her arms across her thin body against the still frosty air, before making for the gate. Groups of people were rallying around, their gazes fixed on the ambulance that had backed up to the main entrance. Beside it was a police van, several men were stripping off and putting on what seemed to be white overalls.

Two police cars parked nearby. In the front of one a tall thin fair-haired woman was talking into a small tape recorder, occasionally turning to a dark-skinned man who was writing; a note book in his hand. For a brief second the woman looked up and stared at Jenny; then went on talking. Workers grouped around, whilst a couple of policemen held them back from the opening doors of the ambulance.

Jenny was suddenly aware of the soft hum of voices had quietened as the ambulance doors opened and she caught the sight of a stretcher being lifted in with what looked like a body shrouded in a plastic bag. Her heart started to beat wildly; there was no need to know whose body it was, as John's car had not moved all night. She turned to the cottage walking quickly, a sense of dark foreboding surrounding her.

Acting D.I Pharies watched the murdered victim disappear into the ambulance and the heavy doors shut tight. She'd witnessed tragic death many times before, life was so fragile, and in the twinkling of an eye with the last breath . . . . nothing.

She'd often mused on the fact that she worried too much and there were never any rewards, but as Jiten had often said. 'The past brings experience and we can only plan for the future. All there really is; is the now.'

She shook her head; coughed and brought herself back to the present moment with all the pieces of jigsaw awaiting her to form a picture of the events at hand.

Someone offered her coffee, it looked strong and inviting, but one sip proved bitter and the taste of the evaporated milk used lingered. She leaned back against the cold metal of the police car, recalling the murder room and what the profiler had said.

Of course she didn't agree with him and wondered what other silly degrees the universities were all about in their quest to make money these days. Reluctantly however Lisa had to agree he had a point when he said that rubbish needed to be disposed of. However, although there might be something in it, there were other more practical theories; like just making sure the victim was dead.

Lisa didn't dwell on the emerging thought that it would have been far easier to shoot him again or just bash him over the head. She placed her half empty cup on the top of the police car and looking around, wondered why she had never been here before.

The river flowed through the centre of town. In fact it was well known from local history that the Danes built the town by the river;

the lands fertile and the woods full of game. The woods at the back of her rose along the inclined hill, dark with oak, beech, poplar and above the skyline; two disused water towers stood like bastions from an earlier age.

'Alright gov?' Jiten's voice startled her and she turned to face him.

'Just thinking' she said eyeing her detective constable. 'Any ideas?'

No one would see the comings and goings at the mill after hours. There was no overtime being worked and the mill was generally closed after six p.m. Lisa was looking past the mill to where the lane finished at a five barred gate. To the left of it, where workers cottages of the past century once stood, only one habitable cottage now remained. The others had now either been demolished completely or had windows broken and boarded up, doors open but hanging on broken hinges, with weeds and small trees finding enough nutriment in the cracked stone paving.

She stiffened at first thinking she was seeing things, but there at the remaining habitable cottage, a figure of a young woman stood. Their eyes met and the figure moved away.

'Who's that?' she exclaimed.

Jiten looked mystified, then followed Lisa's pointing finger. Someone behind Jiten stepped forward a little, uttering

'Thems' the Simkins lass and her lad. Bin there forever, them Simkins.'

Lisa found herself looking at the short plump man who looked well past working years. He didn't wait for her to ask who he was.

'Sam Bretton's the name, me family has a small holding over yonder,' he pointed somewhere towards where the water towers stood. 'Bin on Ravenscroft land forever; so's the Simkins.' Lisa turned away from the obnoxious breath.

'Let's go Jiten,' Lisa's long strides making for the cottage. The gate creaked as she pushed it open, and her sixth sense told her that she'd been watched every step of the way. Her intuition confirmed when the door opened before she had time to knock.

Lisa was confronted by a young woman of indeterminate age and holding a cup of tea; the body and features young and delicate, yet the watchful eyes betraying the wisdom of age.

'Yes?' The soft questioning voice spoke of Cheshire born and bred even in that one word.

Lisa held her ID card in front of her. Jenny glanced at it and to the dark-skinned man behind her and then stepped aside to allow them entrance.

They entered a room that spoke of time past; the stone fireplace and heavy black lintel, to the stone floors and white-washed walls. Lisa felt a nostalgic emotion sweep over her, memories of her grandmother's little three roomed cottage with its stone sink and black oven next to the fire; rice pudding cooking at the bottom and sticks drying out on the top, hand made rag rugs and fly paper hanging everywhere.

The furniture in this room was dark; carved and probably genuine antique as were the copper and brasses, yet everywhere it was as clean as a new pin and with the supple smell of herbs, she felt as if she was surrounded by springtime already with its scents of fresh grass and new flowers. Jenny was the first to ask a question.

'What's happened?'

Lisa stiffened; she wasn't here to give answers but to put the questions. Lisa glanced at Jiten but his face remained passive, leaving her to make the discussion and she had to ask herself if she'd lived alone here, would she like to know there was a murderer at large. In the end her practical side of the investigation won out.

'Sit down'. Lisa pointed to the rocking chair by the fire and watched as the young woman eased a sleepy cat from its bed and sat down stiffly, staring at them with fearful eyes. 'A body has been found on the mill wheel.' There was no other way to say it and Lisa watched Jenny's face turn a shade paler.

'John.' The response was faint, before adding,
'Tilstone.'

'Why do you think it's him?' Lisa edged forward almost afraid the quiet voice would fade away all together.

'His car has been there all night'. The answer was precise and controlled now.

'How do you know?' Jiten said quietly. Both Lisa and Jenny gazed at him questioningly. Then Jenny half-smiled as if explaining the obvious to a small boy.

'I saw it before I went to bed, and it was covered in frost this morning so I concluded the car was never used during the night.'

'And you saw nothing else?' interrupted Lisa, wondering whether Jiten had noticed the frost on the car or was also aware of the fact that she herself had not thought about it.

'No' said Jenny.

'What about the lights being on in the mill.'

'Wouldn't have seem them from here, it's a blank wall facing us.'

Lisa glanced through the small window and saw Jenny was right, but reminded herself to look at the mill from the doorway on the way out, as Ernest's imaginary voice was creeping into her brain saying "Small things lass; small things."

It was then she noticed the ring on Jenny's finger; the unusual design, solid silver, but tarnished by neglect and age. However, what held her attention was its unusual stone and the feeling she had seen or heard about a similar one.

Jenny following Lisa's gaze, and, after passing the cup of tea for D.C. Smith to hold, quickly laid one hand over the other, but too late to stop further questioning.

'Unusual ring Jenny, is it old?' Lisa moved forward making it impossible for Jenny to not acknowledge the question, and slowly Jenny took her covering hand away, showing the colours of the stone reflected by the light. Lisa bent over it and frowned, forgetting for a moment why she was there.

'What's the stone?'

'It's a toadstone,' Jenny answered simply, giving nothing else in the explanation.

'Different,' mused Lisa, straightening up to catch D.C. Smith's eye as he stood, awkwardly holding Jenny's cup of green tea. Lisa stepped aside whilst Jenny sipped again on her hot liquid; the ring put on hold in her mind, as Lisa was now in front on getting answers to her questions.

'So Jenny you didn't see or hear anything unusual during the night or at anytime for that matter'. Jenny shook her head.

'Do you live here on your own?' put in Jiten, his eyes resting on the unwashed plates.

'There's Peter,' Jenny stated quietly.

'Who's Peter and where he is now?' the words from Lisa lashing like a whip, making Jenny gaze in surprise.

'Peter's at school, he's my son.' Lisa coughed, and Jiten turned away.

'So you heard or saw nothing at all out of the normal?'

Jenny shook her head.

Lisa stood up straight and looked at Jiten, who raised his shoulders and eyebrows. But Lisa wasn't done yet, there was something she had to ask, even though it wasn't anything to do with the homicide.

'Why do you live here Jenny? it's a long way from town with neither neighbours nor playmates for Peter.' Jenny gave a slight smile and answered the question like she always did.

'We like it that way, Peter and I.'

Lisa hardly spoke a word as she and Jiten left the cottage and walked over to the car. Jiten sympathetic to her moods didn't start the engine right away but sat there holding the wheel, while Lisa gazed at the row of broken and empty houses; his own thoughts echoing hers.

Was she married? Why had she isolated herself? Where did her income come from? And above all why did the Ravenscrofts allow her to live there, while the adjacent houses had been allowed to become derelict?

Lisa sighed and came back to the practical world. Someone has to keep an eye on Jenny Simkins with a murderer still on the loose. She would have to ask whoever was patrolling the mill to check on Jenny also. 'Poor lass, she must be frightened at the prospect of being there all alone,' she mused.

'Go Smith,' she ordered, lifting her head and leaning back on the seat to release the tension in her shoulders. It surprised her that she felt so alive even with the tension. All her senses were active and the adrenaline now running.

Ernest would have been interested in this case. The information she'd gleaned revolved around in her head, when suddenly a thought struck her. That ring; hadn't Ernest mentioned a ring with a stone called a toadstone. Suddenly it hit her. Ernest had talked about the professor he'd met on the train, who wore a toadstone ring on his finger, and there was no ring on him after he was found murdered. So where did Jenny's ring come from?

Chapter 18

Lisa leaned against the table in the incident room at the police headquarters. After the meeting, when all evidence was assessed and opinions voiced, she felt suddenly drained.

Staring absentmindedly at the litter of coffee cups in the wire trash bin her mind seemed to freeze. So many threads of information, some positive and trustworthy like the pathologist's report, others pointing to alleged happenings with almost 100% certainty and then those loopholes; tiny suggestions hardly worth mentioning but nevertheless there. Each point in the investigation had to be assessed; the conclusion deduced and made as clear as possible to everyone on the case. She knew she mustn't cock up on this one.

Shifting her focus she gazed at the rain hitting the window and forming rivulets. Jenny Simkins could have murdered both the professor and John Tilstone. Lisa shivered; her mother would have said that someone had just walked over her grave . . . .

That thought brought on a frown and a little dry cough as she looked again at the photos on the wall behind her. She'd rather liked Jenny.

The body of Professor Reece stared at her with his glazed dead eyes, the gaping red wound in his neck, reducing him to a butchered animal. Her gaze slid down to the clawed stiff hands, noting the fingers free of any rings. She leaned closer to see if there was any pale ring of skin indicating where a ring may have been, but it was impossible to see with all the blood around. The question that had kept her awake last night kept coming back.

Why would Jenny want the ring? And second and more important; why would she wear it for everyone to see?

The consensus among those in the incident room was that it was too much of a coincidence for there to be two extremely unusual rings, and also that Dr Jeremiah Potts had stated he had seen Jenny in the vicinity of the Saxon Arms. What was puzzling Lisa however was who else could have been at the mill besides John Tilstone?

According to his wife and Hugo Ravenscroft, John was out with an old friend somewhere in Stoke, so Tilstone had lied to them both. Lisa sniffed and pulled out a tissue from a box before blowing on it hard, then staring at it momentarily wondering if she was in for a cold.

'Just my flaming luck,' she mused, sniffing again and throwing the used tissue into the wastebasket. Stopping suddenly, she had a mental vision of something else, and then it was gone. She shook her head.

'Forget the tyre tracks in the frosty ground,' Jitan had informed her, the ambulance, police cars and the doctor has scotched that piece of possible evidence by circling the ground around the mill's entrance.

Lisa found herself not wanting it to be this fragile looking young woman, whose life seemed to be totally dedicated to her only son.

Don't get personal; she reminded herself sighing.

'Now what was the lad's name?' Lisa muttered to herself, her facial features distorting as she scanned her mind for an answer, lips tightly sealed and pulled lengthways, eyebrows knitting together with the effort. Then she had it.

'Peter . . . . of course'. She recalled Jenny Simkins telling her that her son was nine years old, but had failed to mention who the father was. A sudden thought then struck her. Was John Tilstone the father? Was Jenny still having an affair, and had it all got out of hand?

Suddenly Lisa's energy returned; grabbing a pencil from a plastic cup, she flicked open her notepad and wrote quickly. Check how long John Tilstone had worked at the mill, Peter's date of birth, and any rumours of them having an affair. Did Jenny Simkins know Professor Reece and was she seen by anyone else near the Saxon Arms.

Lisa gave a little grin at what yesterday would have seemed a ridiculous thought. Maybe Jenny wasn't so innocent after all. It was now time to find out; time to caution Jenny Simkins and bring her in for detailed questioning. Taking out her mobile, she dialled the officer still at the crime since and told him to bring her everything that was in the waste paper basket in John Tilstone's office at the mill.

Some time later Jenny Simkins sat in a small square room at the police headquarters. Nothing seemed real from the moment the police car had arrived at her cottage to bring her in. First the thin fair-haired detective reading out the arrest warrant, to her screaming that Peter was alone and needed her. Jenny's thoughts were scattered like a large jigsaw puzzle before her. Hugo's car arriving and his insisting Peter went back with him to his home, the Ravens Nest. Her body shaking with the cold, then so heated as if flames of fire had engulfed her.

Lisa recalled Jenny screaming at her that Hugo must not take Peter to the Ravens Nest. Then Dr Potts pushing a needle in her arm and slowly feeling a calmness descend, as she heard voices agreeing that Peter could be looked after at Dr Potts home by his housekeeper for now.

Later, the sedative having worn off, Jenny Simkins and was alone in a small room which had a bed, a toilet and washbasin. She had lain for what seemed an eternity curled up in a foetal position on the hard mattress, her face turned to the wall.

No matter how she tried to move she couldn't. There was no sky or fields, no window to see them. She felt trapped like an animal in a snare. A great fear of darkness descending on her, an eternity of foreboding sweeping into every cell of her body.

Her mother had warned her about the cross-roads in life's journey. Usually to having one's own choices and then living with the consequences. Occasionally however one had no choices; the energy now arraigned against her being the stronger and all the dark powers assembled behind it.

Jenny felt a terrible force and the tightness of this dark energy enfolding her. It spoke in whispers of evil and destruction centuries ago and now biding its time, while it built up its destructive strength.

A great sob escaped her as she pulled the thin blanket over her head and curled up ever more tightly as if the act would help to make her disappear. She tried to bring the face of her mother into her third eye, but all was black and powerless. Then she recalled her mother's voice saying; 'Never allow Peter into the house of a Ravenscroft.'

She shivered with a sudden chill. It had so nearly happened when Hugo had insisted Peter stay with him. That thought panicked her and her heart beat quickly in her chest like a frightened bird.

'Thank God Doctor Potts had seen her distress and came to her rescue. Peter would be safe with him.' she mused.

For a second she relaxed, but only for the darkness to grip her imagination once again. Now that Hugo has her out of the cottage, he could pull it down.

The muffled sobs heard by a female police officer outside her door, reminded her of a rabbit she had once found in a trap. She felt the overwhelming pity of it all and wondered if she was truly cut out for her job. Down the corridor in the chief superintendant's office, acting Detective Inspector Pharies was being congratulated on the arrest. The large oak desk a relic from the past dominated the room and gave grandeur to a plain office. The super leaned back in his chair; his hands clasped.

'Good job Pharies, and you say it was one of our retired DI's who saw this unusual ring on the professor.' His sharp blue eyes never leaving her face. He spread his large hands out on his desk, fingers outstretched, as if to demonstrate where the ring was seen.

'Yes sir' Lisa admitted, though wondering why she didn't really feel that thrilled with herself. The truth being at that moment, she really hated her job.

'Hmm,' the chief superintendant's fingers curled and drummed repeatedly on the shiny surface of his paperless desk; all the time staring at the slim woman in front of him.

Lisa coughed and she shifted her weight from one foot to another, wondering if he would ask her to sit down on the chair in front of his desk, which was now looking more and more inviting.

The hands stopped drumming and he lifted his hands into a cradle position to rest his heavy chin on; his eyes still appraising her achievement.

'I'm testing you Pharies' he stated. 'Don't mess up.' The last words conveying that if she did it would not go well. Not well at all.

With that he stood up, walked over and opened the door. Lisa left his office to be confronted with silence as she walked passed her colleagues desks. Her throat tickled and her face threatened to experience a rush of blood, but she held her head high and made for the coffee machine in the hall; her fingers trembling slightly however, as she lifted the hot cup to her lips.

She needed desperately to talk to Ernest.

Chapter 19

'What's up?'

Detective Constable Smith pulled up a chair beside Lisa. The canteen was almost empty and the remaining waitress leaned against the counter waiting patiently to close up.

Jiten's voice startled Lisa out of her concentration, making her hand shake and spilling coffee over the plastic tablecloth. Absent-mindedly Lisa reached for a tissue and wiped up the liquid and was about to put it into her pocket.

Jiten coughed, bringing her back to reality and causing a flush of embarrassment to her otherwise pale cheeks. She retrieved the soggy tissue and placed it in the centre of the table. The waitress cleared her throat and shuffled her feet impatiently.

'Just thinking,' Lisa said. Leaning back, she stared at Jiten for a moment or two before adding; 'something doesn't seem right.'

She waited; as if by some miracle an explanation to her unease would be offered. None came. She sighed and leaned forward again, suggesting confidentially, 'I just can't see Jenny Simkins cutting anyone's throat.'

'Stranger things have happened,' replied Jiten, his black eyebrows knitting together in an effort to recall an example. Nothing offered itself up, but he'd heard of that saying many times before so there must be something in it. Then suddenly as if inspired he added 'It would depend on how badly she wanted him silenced.' Lisa glared at him.

'You mean done in a fit of passion . . . . not planned.'

Jiten nodded.

She continued 'Whoever it was intended to kill the professor, for they had brought a knife, and the hotel manager had sworn there were none in that room. It was unlikely that the professor had one with him,' continued Lisa.

Jiten took a sip of the lukewarm coffee and the best he could offer Lisa in return was; 'I guess it's our job to find out.'

'Thanks mate.'

For a full five minutes or so they sat silent, their individual thoughts travelling down many avenues, all ending in dead-ends, until the silence was broken by a muffled ring of a cell phone. It took a little while for Lisa to realise the sound was emanating from her own pocket.

'Bugger,' she said looking at the caller's name. Then more out of curiosity than anything else, she answered in a stiff voice. 'Certainly I remember you, Tony something or other isn't it?'

She lifted her eyebrows at Jiten. He cringed and almost felt sorry for the caller, but Lisa was not giving an inch. 'Ah yes; Aubrey the profiler,' her response giving nothing away to take offence over, except perhaps in the way it was said. 'Are you going to tell me we have arrested the wrong person?'

Jiten leaned forward, this was interesting and he didn't want to be left out. Mentally he placed his bets on his superior, but then had second thoughts as Lisa began to chew on her bottom lip.

'So you are saying she wouldn't have used an instrument to shed blood. Not the type. Then what type do; for God's sake?'

Jiten grinned. This was getting good; his bets now swaying towards the profiler. But Lisa had quietened; her voice now a little more controlled. 'Look Aubrey' she was saying. 'Yes I hear you and I admittedly thought along the same lines myself, but . . . . it happens.'

Jiten clenched his fists and was ready to thump the table and about to yell, yes. Now however Lisa's tone became more resigned.

'Alright, I hear what you say, but I'm not hanging around here, I've had enough of lukewarm coffee and bone hard buns.'

Jiten glanced over to the waitress but she was out of hear shot. His mouth dropped a little as he heard Lisa giving the profiler her home address. 'About an hour then, one chance only to convince me and then you are off my patch lad.'

A faint chuckle came out, as Lisa closed her cell phone and stared at Jiten defiantly. 'What?' she asked.

The conversation had thrown her off-course, when Tony Aubrey had suggested the very thing she had been thinking about.

'Anyone who had talked to Jenny would quickly realise she abhorred violence; her life was healing. She could have been in a state of extreme anger or was being threatened; and could have hit someone over the head leading to death. But to actually bring a knife to the scene and slit someone's throat was another matter.'

Tony also suggested they should also talk about what Jenny herself would die for.

'What did she hold dear?' he asked.

Lisa's first thought was Peter. Then all at once however, she realised she needed to talk with someone who had experience in relationships and how they were handled. Her own expertise in that area would have scored a miserable nil.

'Off home Smith,' she said. The waitress at the police headquarters hovered behind their retreating figures with a sigh of relief.

Once on the road Lisa started to relax a little. She liked driving, and once around the roundabout, the road east was quiet, until she turned towards the village of Gelsby. Someone hooted as she braked and turned sharply; forgetting to signal her intentions. She lifted her finger in response, before realising it was not good for her to do that in a police car; she'd had similar feelings when she transferred from uniform branch to her new position.

She relaxed as St Anne's came into view. The old medieval church never changed; unlike life's events. It had stood there since the eleventh century, guarding the village and the village souls. True it had changed from Roman Catholic to Protestant following the Reformation, but that hardly mattered. The building remained the same.

The cottages on either side of the village green hadn't changed much either, since they were built in the seventeen and eighteen centuries, that is apart from the sixteenth century rectory; all a comforting feeling of stability, when the present world seemed to be rushing ahead far too quickly.

A group of locals were standing in the doorway of the Horseshoe. Someone waved and she waved back. Lisa swung to the left at the top end of the green and made another quick left by the side of the inn.

The narrow lane took her past the backs of the cottages to a small parking lot that had been added to address the needs of the modern age. Although no one else did in the force; she locked her car. Her rational being that it would look bad if a detective inspector's car was stolen. Lisa walked up the short narrow path to her back door.

A lump came unexpectedly to her throat. She still hadn't got used to not seeing the light on and finding her mother by the fire waiting for her.

Someone once said there was a difference between a house and a home, and to Lisa a home always had someone waiting there for her.

Once the lights were on she felt better; her coat off, a match to the laid fire and a Chardonnay poured into a large wine glass. Sipping it, she strolled into the hall to pick up the phone. Mobiles were only for mobility as far as Lisa was concerned. She heard it ring out and a man's voice responded.

'Hello?'

It was Ernest's voice. He relied on his friend recognizing it, as he had made a habit of never giving his identity.

'Lisa,' she offered.

'Anything new?' he asked, leaving the question open.

'Just a difficult investigation I can't talk about,' she threw out.

'Recent?' he asked.

'Very'
'Be right over.'

And that's how it always was, and it suited them both. It kept Ernest's mind ticking over and Lisa gaining in experience from her retired boss. For a person who disliked exercise and had to be coached by his wife to walk around the village; he appeared at Lisa's front door in two minutes flat, or so it seemed.

The normal procedure was maintained. Ernest had a glass filled with Glenfidic and Lisa her usual white wine; a plate of Cadbury's chocolate biscuits and two arm chairs by the fire, and all before Lisa broached the subject of the ring.

'You said the prof was wearing a ring.'

Ernest laid his whisky down on the hearth. 'Yes, an unusual ring called a toadstone.'

'What are the chances of us coming across two such rings?' asked Lisa.

'Can happen.' Ernest held her gaze letting her come up with her response.

'But highly unusual, right?'

Just then the door bell rang and after a few moments Lisa came back with a tall young man who, without hesitation walked over to Ernest holding out his hand.

'Tony Aubrey sir.' He clasped Ernest's hand in a firm handshake. 'Pleased to meet you. I've heard a lot about your successful cases; it's a pleasure to make your acquaintance.'

Ernest sat down a little taken aback. How come he felt at a disadvantage.

'Tony is a profiler,' announced Lisa, turning her back on them to pour out a drink for her guest. Tony indicated with his fingers the amount of single malt and turned to Ernest, whose face still registered disbelief. Profilers, the ones he'd dismissed as a waste of university time and money; looked like ferrets; all shifty eyed, as though that were constantly analyzing everyone. However confronting him was a tall good looking man.

'Profiler is a police name; I studied human psychology trying to understand how personalities would react in different circumstances.' Lisa was about to chip in, but refrained as Ernest held up his hand.

'You're telling me you can always tell what a person would do.' The disbelief in Ernest's tone was marked, which made Lisa feel better.

'No sir,' he pulled up a high backed chair and sat down, nursing the golden liquid. 'Not always, no one can really tell how someone will react, but let me put this to you. Say you knew someone who was very shy and timid and always found himself being bullied, what would he do?'

'Run away.' suggested Ernest, clearly not too impressed.

'Most times you would be right, but it's been known that if their fear was great enough, they could lose control and lash out to the point of killing their tormentor.'

Lisa and Ernest looked at each other remembering a similar case where a youth had hit his dominating father with a hammer and killed him. The conversation continued with questions and suggestions, but both Ernest and Lisa never heard Tony say it always happened that way. It was the odds that helped in a profiler's casebook. In the end a certain respect had been established and both Lisa and Ernest found themselves liking the young man.

'So Tony, what would your assessment be of Jenny Simkins cutting someone's throat?'

Tony turned his glass around watching the colours in the liquid from the firelight.

'What is the thing that's most important to her?'

'The cottage.' Lisa offered.

'Is it?' Tony turned and looked into her eyes. 'What would be most important to you?'

She felt it, first in her heart then in the whole of her body. The answer was, without question, as it had been since time began.

'My child . . . .' but then quickly added; 'if I had one.'

Tony looked at Ernest.

'Peter?' Ernest questioned, then adding; 'would you kill for Peter?

The profiler frowned. 'The odds are for, but not everyone is the same. But then my question to that would be; is Peter also important to someone else.'

Chapter 20

Ernest folded his newspaper and let it fall on the floor beside him. It wasn't from lack of interest in world affairs but from the fact he just couldn't concentrate.

He let his head fall backwards against the soft leather chair and closed his eyes, listening to the sounds from the kitchen. Normally it would have brought the feeling of deep satisfaction and relaxation. Yet today they were just background noises interrupting a pattern of thought he was pursuing.

He closed his eyes trying hard to blank out any thoughts that were hindering his concentration, but gave up finally as all he could think about was the ring the professor wore. 'Was it a clue or just a coincidence?' he pondered, frowning slightly.

The phone rang. He jumped up too quickly feeling a little wobbly as the blood had drained from his head, and he made for the hall.

'Yes?' He listened with a frown of annoyance on his face and looked at Rita, who had appeared by the doorway and mouthed the word 'Ted.'

She raised her eyebrows and disappeared quickly closing the kitchen door behind her. Ernest listened to the monotone voice asking if Lisa was at his house. He answered truthfully; he hadn't a clue where she was. Ted went on about she should give him her mobile number.

Ernest let the phone slip away from his ear; a resigned look swept over his face, and wondered whether he should sit on the stairs, as his legs were getting tired. Thankfully Ted decided to put the phone down himself.

Rita's face appeared, pushing the door open with her foot and holding out two steaming cups of coffee and beckoning with her head towards the lounge. No one spoke for a while. They had settled down by the flickering flame of the fire; the warmth of the cups in their hands holding them in suspense.

The clock on the mantelpiece seemed to tick louder than normal as if waiting for a certain passage of time before another path in life was forged. Rita looked up.

'Tell me again about this chap you met on the train that got murdered.'

Ernest shrugged his shoulders. 'Not much to tell love; he seemed intelligent and pleasant enough I dare say.'

Rita placed her cup on the tiled hearth and wrapped her overly large cardigan around herself, before letting him continue.

'Professor of late medieval history taught at Oxford, I believe.'

'Married?' asked Rita. He shrugged his shoulders.

'Lisa didn't say anything about him being married, just that he lived alone in Oxford and still spent time at the university, although he was retired.'

'Anything else?' asked Rita.

He shook his head, eyeing his wife with interest. She was taking him somewhere; his very bones felt it, causing a shiver of excitement to run through him. Every case he'd ever worked on had brought on the same feeling. His hands shook a little and he stared at the liquid in the cup.

'We need to know far more about these rings called toadstones,' stated Ernest; sitting up straight.

'The library?' he asked; looking at her for confirmation it was the best source.

'The computer, surely . . . .' Rita replied, at which Ernest flopped back again as if the wind had been taken out of his sails.

He knew she was right, but it didn't help that flutter of panic that had first started when computers were introduced in his work area. Fortunately he was near retirement and didn't suffer the strain he'd seen some of the others go though. He'd never brought one although Lisa had tried on many occasions to get him interested and, truth to tell, he'd even considered getting one, but then Rita came back into his life.

Rita on the other hand had adapted well as the new computer age entered the hospitals and she had already bought one, while Ernest would only talk about it. For now however she kept her silence and her mind probed other possible avenues.

'Oxford then,' she cried; the excitement in her voice rising.

'What?' her spouse stared at her blankly.

'Oxford, Ernest.' She took his hand in hers, and gazed at him; her blue eyes lit with energy. 'Let's take a trip to Oxford love.' She was now on a roll and her words followed swiftly.

'We could talk to people who knew the professor personally: 'What was he like? What he did in his spare time after he retired? If they didn't know about toadstones, who would? Then of course there's always the Bodleian library at the university.'

Rita stopped and looked at him for some sign of agreement and when he nodded, she clapped her hands.

'Right then, train times . . . ?' She got up, the full force of her organizational skills coming into play. 'Get hold of Lisa and get all the info. you can on what is known about the prof.'

It was all going too quickly and Ernest wondered if they were overstepping the mark a little. The powers that be at the police headquarters wouldn't be too pleased about any interference in one of their cases, even if he was a former detective inspector. But the thought didn't last long; his mind already on the questions he needed answers to.

He picked up the phone and Lisa responded, recognizing the caller's number on her call display.

'Lisa Pharies,' she said.

They chatted for a long time, not realising that the engaged signal from her phone was frustrating Ted more and more.

When Ted's car pulled up at the same time with a squeal of brakes outside Lisa's; one or two front doors opened and empty milk bottles put out; even though the milk-man had long since gone for the day.

Lisa feeling better after talking to her mentor, didn't feel at all bad about telling Ted a lie about being in the shower when he'd phoned. Apart from the occasional whiff of manure, her time spent with him had been reasonably satisfying. After all, she was only human she told herself after he had gone, and needs were needs.

Ted slid into his car seat with a smile on his face, he was pleased to hear that Ernest and Rita were taking a brief vacation and that Lisa was still extremely responsive to his prowess; not that he'd ever had any doubt in that area. Farmers learn at an early age what the equipment nature had given them was all about.

However Ted had the sense to back off when he'd seen the look on her face, when he said he could have told her it was Jenny Simkins all along. Time would tell.

'Let her feel miserable and she'd soon learn that women were meant to look after the home; not play at detectives,' he mused to himself.

Rita, in the meantime while waiting for their taxi to arrive, had switched on her computer, filled a large glass with white wine and settled down to study anything that came up on Google about toadstones

Most of the referenced material pertained to a small bone being found in the head of toad. The toad going through many rituals in earlier centuries before it was extracted. It was supposed to have many magical powers and was greatly valued and taking on the name of a toadstone.

Another reference stated that the great ERASMUS (1465-1536) saw a toadstone at the feet of the statue of the Virgin Mary at the "Virgin in Walsingham" shine.

Nothing much to go on there, unless the professor belonged to some witches coven and she very much doubted that; he was far too educated for that.

'Better look to Peter,' Rita mused, as Tony Aubrey had suggested, which brought her to the obvious question.

'Who was Peter's father?'

Surely someone around the area knew, after all there were a lot of fellows working at the mill and people gossiped. The thought struck her that maybe Jenny had been raped, but then realized she was now grasping at straws. Shutting down the computer, Rita sat back and stared at the blank screen.

About four pm, a town taxi pulled up outside Ernest's cottage. A few curtains moved in the windows of their neighbours. Two taxis at the same door in a week was worthy of a comment or two later.

Chapter 21

Lisa awoke feeling energized. The sleeping tablets had done the trick and had given her that long needed good night's sleep.

Her mind was slowly filing bits of evidence together and she was anxious to try out her theories. Also the sun had made one of its rare appearances, which always lifted her spirits. So in a positive frame of mind Lisa set off for the police headquarters.

Heads lifted up from their computers and eyes followed the acting detective inspector as she made her way past the clutter of desks and the screens that defined the work space of her colleagues to the fully enclosed office space that she was now allowed to use.

Her eyes drifted along the thin corridor to the chief superintendant's office and wondered how long the powers that be would continue to give her his support. She stopped by the coffee machine recalling the umpteen cups of coffee she'd made for Ernest from an old electric kettle. In those days it was a jar of instant coffee with fresh milk and a plate of biscuits to boot. All free.

Jiten was standing by her desk waving a file at her and mouthing something she didn't understand, but knew it was important.

Taking the file from him she opened it and read with interest the autopsy report on John Tilstone. Cause of death:—A bullet wound through the neck causing massive haemorrhaging.

Lisa's eyes flicked down the page, he had seemed to be in good health apart from a rash around his genitals. She coughed and murmured 'Looks like our John played the field.' She read it out loud.

'Motive—jealousy?' questioned Jiten straightening up

Lifting an eyebrow Lisa shrugged, 'It has happened many times before.'

She pulled out the other folder tucked beneath it and sat down in her chair to read it. It was about Jenny Simkins. Lisa summarized each word as her eyes skimmed the report.

Jenny Simkins was born in the mill cottage. Lived with her mother; the local midwife. No father mentioned. Jenny got pregnant, aged fifteen. Again no father mentioned.

Lisa looked up biting her bottom lip.

'So why did Jenny and her son Peter carry on living at the mill cottage, after the other cottages were either demolished or vacated and allowed to deteriorate beyond repair?'

Jiten shrugged his shoulders adding, 'food for thought.'

They stared at each other for awhile. Then Lisa thumped her hand down hard on the files. 'Too many jigsaw pieces here, but I'm convinced they're all from the same puzzle.' She read the file again carefully.

'Seems Sara Simkins was a midwife and had nursed Hugo's mother till she died. Maybe that was the reason,' said Jiten; offering the suggestion. 'so where was Sara Simkins trained; they must know something about her.'

Lisa's look could have sunk the Titanic.

'This is rural Cheshire; not many doctors, and small cottage hospitals. Even in my childhood there was always someone whose skills were passed down and used when needed. Sara Simkins was probably more experienced than the ones that trained in nursing schools. Probably laid out the dead too.' before adding, 'Life and death was a family matter; personal like.'

Jiten nodded; remembering his own life in an Indian village.

Lisa had the feeling there was an interesting story behind the Simkins family; both past and present. 'Time to talk to the Ravenscrofts.'

She flicked quickly through her list of phone numbers and dialled. It was picked up; she glanced up at the dusky face of her constable and winked.

'Detective Inspector Pharies here and I would like to talk with you.' She paused, then adding, 'half an hour, that will be great; and I would be grateful if your sister could be there also.'

But before leaving Lisa clicked onto Google Earth and scanned the area around the mill and the course of the river. She then clicked onto the internet and studied the surprisingly large amount of information on the mill. There was an old picture of the cottages before most of them had fallen into disrepair. Leaning over the gate at the end cottage was a small woman in a poke bonnet and a shawl around her shoulders: In the doorway a small barefooted girl. Lisa had no doubt that they were Simkins and suddenly felt that she was not only dealing with a murder but with time itself.

Ravens Nest was an imposing red brick Victorian house, its large iron gates now permanently standing open and the hinges rusting.

However its large impressive front door; solid oak with black iron hinges recently painted a shiny black. The very door structure suggesting one would be confronted and greeted by a maid or butler. Lisa couldn't help recalling the feeling of inferiority of her own circumstances she'd suffered from as a child, being brought up in an old two bed-roomed terraced house.

But, after driving there with her constable, it was no servant that opened the door but Hugo Ravescroft himself. He stepped aside to lead them into a rather dark panelled hallway; the only colour was a large bowl of rhododendrons gracing an antique carved chest. The brass on the antique swords displayed on the wall was unpolished with patches of green verdigris between the cracks in the metal. Jiten stopped awhile to admire an ancient pistol only to be prodded by a finger as Lisa was walking past him, following Hugo down the hallway.

The room they entered was pleasant, its large bay window giving lots of light. The room was dominated by a massive marble fireplace, the centrepiece of which was carved out in the shape of a bird holding a stalk of wheat in its beak. Above it an oil painting of a man who gave no doubt as to his identity; Kristen's face bearing many of the same features. Neither could be called handsome with their small beady dark eyes; faces not forgotten once seen. Kristen Tilstone sat on a chair: her back straight, eyes red and face pale.

'Drink?' Hugo's voice brought Lisa back to the present. Both she and Jiten declined, making it obvious this was not a social call. Hugo helped himself to a whisky and handed his sister a dark sherry before offering seating.

Again Lisa declined. Jiten was studying the room; its past displayed everywhere and he would have loved to have looked around more. Antiques were interesting to him, especially as his grandfather had ran an antique stall back in India.

Lisa spoke. 'This won't take long Mr Ravenscroft, just some loose ends to tie up.' She glanced at his sister who had hardly moved and looked pale. Hugo sat on the arm of a big solid armchair, sending signals of a totally conscience-free individual. Suddenly it was Kristen that spoke causing all of them to gaze at her.

'It's about my John, isn't it? Has that girl been charged?' There was hope mingled with contempt in her voice. At the same time Lisa was aware of Hugo's knuckles tightening around his glass and his sudden intake of breath.

"Strike whilst the iron's hot," Ernest would have said and before Lisa could think about the reasons for her visit, she turned to Hugo and shot out with. 'Is Peter yours?'

Had Hugo's glass been thinner, it would have broke, so tight was his grip. Kriston gasped and the pause that followed made the ticking of the clock so very loud. At last the eruption came.

'Christ. Is this what it's all about? the boy Simkins' parentage and you have decided it's me,' said Hugo.

Kriston gave a small sound like an animal in pain, her hand shook spilling some of the sherry. Lisa's eyes flicked from brother to sister watching their faces, but couldn't detect any signs of their lying.

'Just something that needed to be ruled out, no offence. You see I couldn't understand why the Simkins were allowed to remain in the cottage.'

There was visible relief emanating from Hugo, he got up and went to stand the fire place. 'My father,' he said looking up at the portrait behind him, 'wanted a son more than anything else in the world'. Kristen looked up at her brother; a sad smile on her lips.

'And,' he carried on, 'when my mother was in labour, Sara Simkins cared for her; her reputation outshining any doctor's for safe births. However . . .' he slowed down, as if trying to visualise his own emergence from the womb. 'Things didn't go to well and it was a choice between saving the baby or the mother . . .' his voice tailing off.

Lisa stepped in quickly. 'So she put her energies into saving you.' He nodded; something akin to a tear glazed his eyes and his voice choked a little.

'My mother died.'

Lisa was at a loss for words and just stared at him, wondering how one lived with the fact his birth had killed his mother. Kristen took up the saga.

'It was father who had told Sara Simkins to save his son's life over his wife's. The baby was choking and my mother was haemorrhaging badly.' Kristen's voice was monotone, as if repeating something devoid of feelings. Hugo then added; 'the midwife said she would, but only on one condition and my father granted it.' Lisa cut in, 'that she and her descendants could stay in the cottage?'

Kristen nodded.

'Why didn't Sara ask to own the cottage outright?' added Jiten, stepping in with a question that Lisa that was about to ask.

'She didn't want it that way. It was just for her and her descendants to live in,' added Hugo; quoting the words of the original pact agreed to.

'Not just for her life time then; but looking further ahead into the future,' added Jiten, pausing with a frown. 'Seems a bit odd don't you think. They were very old cottages even then and the council could step in with a demolition order anytime.' It was a long sentence for Jiten and all eyes were focussed on him.

'This is England, and my own terraced house is probably older,' said Lisa as she turned towards the brother and sister. 'Thanks for clearing that up, it must have been painful for you both.' Lisa held her hand out in genuine sympathy as they said their goodbyes.

Once in the car, Lisa suddenly said. 'She must have been fair-haired.'

Jiten turn his head, looking quizzically at his companion.

'Eyes on the road,' she ordered; then answered his own unasked question.

'Hugo's mother must have been fair, as Hugo looks nothing like his father and sister. I wonder if his father saw the woman he let die, every time he looked at his son.'

Jiten kept quiet and concentrated on the traffic.

Lisa leaned back thinking about Henry VIII; it seemed both men had been willing to sacrifice their wives for a son.

Chapter 22

The same faces hiding behind the net curtains that had watched Ernest and his wife leave a few days ago, now watched their return. Rumour had it they had been to Canada and were thinking of emigrating, that was until someone had informed them that the taxi driver said they had been to Oxford, leaving the query why?; nothing of interest there but the University and neither were the academic type. Curtains flicked again to get a better view of Lisa hurrying to greet the home-comers.

'So what did you discover?' asked Lisa a little out of breath. She had hardly allowed Ernest and Rita to put down their bags in the hall before she again cornered them with questions. Ernest raised a hand. 'Hold on there lass'. He grinned and glanced at his wife for support before turning to Lisa. 'Food first young lady; never could think on an empty stomach.'

'Don't look to me to satisfy it,' said Rita, calling from half way up the stairs.

Lisa sighed and muttered to herself; 'if this is what married life is all about; forget it.' Then she heard Ernest chuckling as he replied; 'Guess that means a meal at the Horseshoe then.'

Lisa knew she would never get the hang of this thing called wedded bliss, but the thought of a huge plate of fish and chips warmed her insides.

Half and hour later the three of them were tucking into freshly fried cod and chips with a huge dollop of mushy peas; a plate of cherry pie and coffee to follow satisfied their hunger pains. Lisa sat back; now eager to stimulate her brain. 'Okay, now let's have the real gravy from your visit to Oxford.'

Ernest glanced at his wife and winked. Lisa froze, hoping that they were not coming up with yet another excuse to keep her in the dark. Ernest again frustrated her as he beckoned to the waiter for three glasses of ale, testing her patience to the limit by waiting until he'd taken a long swig of the beer he'd ordered, before breaking the mounting tension. Lisa need not have worried however, as they were just as eager to pass on their information, as she was to hear it.

'We had a lucky break,' he said, looking over admiringly at his wife before proceeding. One of the professors we met with was more than willing to tell us all he knew about his colleague Professor Reece, when it turned out that Rita had previously nursed one of the professor's Canadian relatives.

Rita picked up the story and added, 'seems our Professor Reese was obsessed with his ancestry, and a guy called Matthew Hopkins.'

Lisa frowned; she didn't want to hear about the guy's hobbies for goodness sake.

Lisa glanced at Rita, who was at that moment beckoning to someone standing in the half hidden doorway of the Inn. Rita got up to make room for her guest Tony Aubrey, who then seated himself between Rita and Ernest.

Lisa's irritation with the presence of the police profiler must have shown, as she continued to ignore the presence of this newcomer at the table. Impatiently Lisa waited for Ernest to continue; knowing there must be more.

'Matthew Hopkins was the Witch Finder General in the sixteen hundreds,' Ernest said quietly, with half a smile on his face. Both Lisa and Tony waited for him to continue, wondering what the heck this Matthew Hopkins had to do with the homicides and where all this was leading.

It was Rita who responded. 'Our informant hinted that Professor Reese was in possession of the diaries of Matthew Hopkins, and had even traced his own ancestry back to him.'

Again they stared at her in confusion, waiting for further clarification. Rita looked at Ernest for help. He moved forward, circling his large hands around his glass, before adding; 'I kept asking myself; what was the information the professor had, that brought him to our town and got himself killed over?'

There was silence before Lisa spoke. 'Do you really think that the contents of his briefcase held information that was important; so important in fact, that someone in this day and age would even kill for?'

Ernest looked at her almost with concern in his eyes before adding; 'never leave a stone unturned; it could have been used as a motive for blackmail maybe.'

Lisa stared at him, wondering if this was the reason why detectives were generally retired early; their ideas in solving crime scenes getting more and more fanciful.

'So Rita and I concentrated our research on this Matthew Hopkins character and it was surprising what we found,' continued Ernest.

'And what was that?' Up to this point Tony Aubrey had not said a word. Lisa turned to him in surprise, as if she'd just realized he was there and Tony was visibly blushing.

Ernest continued. 'The extermination of the so-called witches started around 1484 by the Pope and at that time over fifty thousand people were accused of witchcraft. Then when James 1 came to the throne, the practice was taken up in England with a vengeance; although I believe the numbers were much less and most of it happening in Essex. Matthew Hopkins, it seems, was a fanatical puritan and had a reputation for discovering so-called witches. His methods were extreme and cruel and for this, he was recognised and appointed Witch Finder General by King James.'

By this time Ernest had everyone's full attention, until Liza broke the spell. She had listened patiently for awhile but could stand it no longer.

'Sod it Ernest, we are investigating a murder here; not a guy who liked to hunt for witches.'

They all looked at her as though she had missed the point being made. It was Rita who replied. 'Lisa, if the professor was interested in witchcraft, it was maybe something to do with witchcraft that had brought him to Cheshire in the first place.'

Lisa looked bewildered for a moment, and then asked sarcastically. 'Are you telling me there's a witch's coven here in the town; with witches who dance naked around a fire?' She laughed out loud. 'Aye maybe when the druggies get tanked up on Guy Fawkes Night; but witches? No way.'

Her loud laugh brought looks of surprise and astonishment from the other tables around the room. Ernest unaffected by her ridicule waited for her to calm down before continuing.

'I'm not suggesting anything love, but Rita and I followed up on our research of this Matthew Hopkins and his activities in this area as well and,' he paused for a moment, and looked at her pointedly; before adding 'We did discover something that's well worth further investigation here.'

Taking a long drink from her glass to stop an irritating nervous cough, Lisa stared at him and whispered,

'Go on.'

Now all the four occupants around the table moved together, closing ranks some would say, as Rita took over the unfolding story after Ernest nodded in her direction.

'A long time ago in the sixteen hundreds, the land that the Ravenscroft's now hold once belonged to the Simkins family; a Ralph and Beth Simkins to be exact.' Rita waited for some sign of surprise, but none came. 'It appears that the two families owned adjoining land, the only difference being the river that ran through the Simkins's land gave them good harvests. After a couple of very dry years, the Ravenscrofts had poor harvests and lost money, so they accused the Simkins of witchcraft.'

Lisa sat up and sniffed. 'You can't accuse any one of witchcraft for poor harvests; anyone would know it was the river that made the difference.'

Looking unperturbed; Rita continued. 'Maybe, but when cows are poisoned and pigs get sick, but never on the Simkins land; some people get funny ideas.'

Nothing was added for a while to let it sink in, and then Tony Arbury asked. 'Did this Beth Simkins have a reputation for herbal cures and such like?'

Rita nodded before adding: 'She also had an old nurse who used unorthodox methods; and when the Ralph Simkins died later for no apparent reason, all eyes turned to Beth, his young wife.'

'What was the nurse's name?' asked Tony having nothing better to say, and was surprised when Ernest regarded the question with interest, but shrugged his shoulders.

Lisa pushed her glass forward and demanded; 'I need another drink,' to which Tony, taking the hint; raised four fingers at the waiter.

'What the dickens has all this got to do with the prof. having his throat cut.' asked Lisa. 'Gee folks, all this was hundreds of years ago for goodness sake.'

Ernest sighed. 'Lisa, the only thing that could have brought Professor Reese to the town was to do with the Ravenscroft and Simkins. He had the time and the passion once retired.' He paused, as if to let it sink in again before adding; 'and he was wearing a ring that was also very popular during that period in the sixteenth century.'

All at once Lisa's mind did an about-turn. 'The ring Jenny Simkins has?'

'Maybe, but we have to establish if it was the same one lass, you can't go accusing people on hopeful evidence,' replied Ernest.

'Well, tell me who can then?' Lisa replied. She was almost going to add, 'clever clogs,' but refrained and blushed.

'I can.' Silence followed Ernest's blunt retort. Time seemed to stop. Then almost in unison the cry came.

'How?'

'Not every marking on the stone can be the same, remember myths would have us believe they were supposed to have come out of the heads of toads, and each would likely be slightly different; especially in the way they were cleaned, processed and indeed mounted.' Ernest then turned to Lisa.

'Let me examine Jenny Simkins' ring. I've got a feeling I would be able to identify if it was Professor Reese's.'

Tony followed asking a very practical question, 'Would that do anything towards securing Jenny's release?'

'Possibly,' agreed Ernest, 'and that would send us down another path that might well bring other surprises.'

Lisa picked up on the "us", and was surprised she was not upset and annoyed. It felt good to have the experience of others giving a little help. Gaining confidence, she told them all about the interview with the Ravenscroft family. But the only comments she got back were ones she had already thought about, apart from the last one that is, when she mentioned. 'Hugo's father desperately wanted the land to stay in Ravenscroft hands, hence his need for a son; just like Henry V111.'

The police profiler then added another interesting thought of his own.

'Yes, Hugo would be afraid of marriage, in case his own wife might die in childbirth. He must have always felt quite guilty at being the cause of his own mother's death.'

Chapter 23

Lisa glanced at a plastic bag of Ted's dirty washing, and wondered if he had forgotten to take it with him after he'd changed there last evening. He hadn't mentioned that he would be going into town where the launderette was. She could have given him some of her own washing to take too had she known.

Half way up the narrow staircase she froze, remembering that the only launderette in town had closed six months ago. God forbid, did he expect her to do his washing? The sudden rush of adrenaline caused her shoulders to tense up. Her hand gripped the hand rail as she pounded up the stairs to her bedroom.

Plonking herself down on the unmade bed she took a deep breath and sat awhile staring into space before gathering her thoughts again and retrieving a scrap of paper she had previously tucked under the alarm clock: her eyes flicking to and fro as she read the listed items one by one.

Pick up a good bottle of wine and meat pie.

Let Ernest examine Jenny's ring.

Talk to Dr Potts, re: State of Jenny Simkins mental health

'Right, first things first,' she said to herself, recalling her mother's advice. Digging into her jacket pocket she pulled out her purse and emptied the contents onto the bed. A quick glance confirmed she had enough cash for a good bottle of wine and a pie.

Next she dialled two numbers, spending less than a few minutes in conversation with each and sat back satisfied. The constable in charge in the evidence room would have the Reece and Simkins articles ready for identification in an hour, and the second call confirmed her appointment with Doctor Potts, who would be delighted to give her any help he could after his morning calls.

Acting D.I. Pharies was beginning to see some permanency to her title. The ring would belong to the professor and Dr Potts would confirm Jenny Simkins unstable state of mind. Now all she had to do was to get a quick confession and discover where the knife and gun were, which she admitted could be a marathon job in itself with large areas of woodland to cover; not to mention the river. The latter had already come up with a lot of old discarded metal but no gun or knife.

There was that odd moment of regret, knowing that Peter was now without his mother; but it was good to know that the doctor had stepped in and his schooling wasn't going to be interrupted.

Lisa sighed, still slightly in conflict with her true feelings and hating her job. She recalled Ernest's advice coming loud and clear to her again and again. "Don't let yourself get emotionally involved; it's been the destruction of many a fine detective."

She sighed again, and wondered if Ernest would have felt the same about Rita, had she not gone to Canada.

It had certainly left him devoid of any real loving relationships for over half his life.

An hour later however, Ernest was showing a lot of emotion; his eyes bright and face flushed as he handed her the ring back.

'That's not the Professor Reeve's ring,' he stated bluntly.

Lisa blinked in disbelief. 'Oh come on Ernest, how the bloody hell can you be so sure.'

He took the ring off her again and held it up, beckoning Lisa to stand by his side. 'This ring is mottled, with a slight green and light brown colouration.' He moved out of her way as she leaned closer. 'Now can you see anything that draws your eye to it?'

Lisa, straining her neck in the process of getting a closer look, replied. 'Not really; just the two green and brown colours merging together.'

'Precisely,' said Ernest excitedly. 'The professor's ring had a bluish spot that reminded me of an eye, and there was a fine line in the left hand corner,' he added with conviction.

'Honestly Ernest, you mean to say you remembered all that after only a moment's look at the dammed ring.' The sarcasm in Lisa's voice was pronounced but Ernest seemed unaware of it, as he lowered his hand and placed the ring back in its labelled box. 'That's not the professor's ring and I'll stake my reputation on it.'

The police constable hovering in the background smiled to himself. He was getting close to retirement and hadn't much time for these young know-it-all detectives with all their schooling. Nine times out of ten they had to go back to the drawing board with their ideas so to speak; while detectives of his generation used their eyes and wits and learnt on the job.

Ernest patted Lisa's shoulder and felt it stiffen. 'Coffee luv?' he suggested, and she nodded feeling fully deflated.

Over coffee in a quiet corner, Ernest's mood changed from that of achievement into brooding; with Lisa scanning his face over the rim of her cup.

'What now?' she asked at length, knowing his moods; like the weather man knows changing cloud patterns.

Ernest didn't answer for a while, and then put his plastic cup down. 'Go and hear what Dr Potts has to say about Jenny Simkins. He's not only a medical doctor, but an amateur archaeologist and a historian as well.' He took another sip; grimacing at the awful taste of the coffee from the coffee machine before adding, 'ask him a little more about Peter's birth. Was it only Jenny's mother who delivered Peter, or was he there too?'

Lisa looked up; puzzlement showing in her face.

'Every corner Lisa; every corner,' Ernest reminded her and; as an afterthought added: 'Come for supper. Does roast beef and all the trimmings sound good?'

'Yes, thanks Ernest.'

Lisa laid her hand over his, failing to feel the sudden tension as Ernest realised that Rita might have other ideas about what was on the evening menu.

Driving home with a nice round of beef, he wasn't at all ashamed of trying to use dinner tactics to find out more about how her interview with the doctor went. He whistled a nifty tune from the sixties; slowing down as he neared his cottage and waving at a shifting curtain. His one effort now was to convince Rita that a roast beef dinner was somewhat of a necessity.

In the meantime Lisa avoided her superintendent; with a sideways disappearing act, whenever he appeared. After spending the last half hour in the canteen contemplating a chocolate donut, she checked her watch as she saw Detective Constable Smith approaching.

Dr Potts' house cum surgery, was a Victorian structure; big, square, with gables and columns around the imposing front door. The walled garden was not overly large but very private with a red brick wall running all the way around.

The front wall of the house was adjacent to the pavement, and two large iron gates supporting the doctor's brass plate, a flagged path led up to the main entrance of the house. This same entrance served the doctors private patients as well as visitors; leaving the National Health patients to use the side entrance that led to a prefabricated room that had been added in the early nineteen fifties.

Lisa knocked on the front door and was greeted by a middle aged well preserved housekeeper. She and the detective constable were shown into the parlour that served the private patients when needed;

the name of the room didn't change in these old houses, giving it a touch of elegance. Bay windows overlooked the neatly trimmed lawns and ivy clad red brick walls and a sundial tried its best to find the sun under a large oak tree that covered the ground in shadow.

The original fire place had been modernised by the addition of an artificial log fire. It was a cheerful room and spoke of good taste. Lisa's admiration was interrupted by the door opening and Dr Potts entering.

He came forward offering his hand in a warm greeting, and indicated two chairs that were comfortably arranged for a chat.

The housekeeper appeared with a trolley bearing bone china crockery; tea, coffee and biscuits.

Dr Potts remained standing; leaning against the fireplace mantel and fingering a small jade ornament which sat on it. Lisa had seen this type of posturing before in an earlier interview with Hugo Ravenscroft and it raised her hackles. It spoke of dominance.

'Don't be intimidated,' Lisa told herself. She leaned forward accepting the tea but refusing the biscuits as a gesture she was still in control. She came straight to the point.

'Dr Potts, I believe that you are Jenny Simkins' medical doctor.'

The doctor half smiled. 'You could say that, but in reality apart from her pregnancy and the birth of her son, I've never been called out to attend her.'

Lisa found herself surprised that the doctor had been there at the birth of Jenny's son, seeing that Jenny's own mother was the midwife. The doctor seemed to read her mind. 'She needed a forceps delivery and stitches,' he offered, 'the girl was young and very small boned.' Lisa understood and nodded. She took a sip of the surprisingly good tea.

'And how would you assess Jenny Simkins,' she asked bluntly. 'Would say she was mentally fit in every way?'

The doctor was quiet for the longest time, looking down at his feet as if considering what to say and how to do it. He shuffled his feet and tapped the mantle shelf. 'She's what our ancestors would have called fey!'

Lisa nodded and Jiten looked at her curiously, feeling out of his depth when old Cheshire families often used years-old words and expressions of their own. Lisa must have felt his discomfort for she turned to him saying; 'a little simple, if you pardon my use of words.'

He nodded and sighed. Then the doctor seemed to come into his own as he straightened up.

'Peter is doing well here, and he's intelligent. It's a bad time for him as exams are looming that could effect his future.' He considered his wording before further expounding his feelings; 'I brought him into the world and feel some responsibility I guess.'

Lisa felt almost sorry that she had to burst his bubble; Peter had no doubt brought a new aspect into the doctor's life. Lisa added, 'it seems new evidence has come to light and it appears we now have little evidence against the Simkins woman.'

The stunned look on Dr Potts face took them both by surprise. He looked visibly shaken.

'You mean she will be released?' he said in disbelief.

Lisa stood up, followed by Jiten; after putting down his half eaten biscuit. 'We have no evidence to convict her of murder,' she repeated.

'But what was she doing near the Saxon arms?' the Doctor asked stunned. Lisa shrugged her shoulders and added. 'That's not enough to convict her.'

On the way back Jiten was quiet, knowing his boss had to have space to think things through. Many minutes passed before she ventured her thoughts.

'What was the real reason the doctor wanted to bring up Peter?' Then a thought struck her. 'Although the doctor was old enough to be Jenny's father, it hadn't deterred others from doing something they would later be ashamed of.'

Chapter 24

Ted had popped in for a while but left early; milking time was not something that could be put off or put on-hold on the farm. Ted for a change was quite thoughtful and listened to her concerns and didn't annoy her once. Lisa had begun to think two people living together could be something worth considering.

Humming a little tune, she sat down in front of her computer and brought up her report. She stared at it in disbelief, instead of looking at her wording; there was a message in the top left hand corner that read:

> *Thought I'd give you a hand by correcting your spelling and paragraphing. I suggest you use Arial as it looks so much better. Love, Ted.*

She felt sick, the juices in her stomach churned violently. 'How dare he,' she muttered to herself. It was bad enough his going into her personal files; but to change them!

Lisa clinched her fist and banged it down hard on the table, before re-reading the text and calming down. Her eyes scanned the sentences, and then reluctantly agreed that it looked much more professional and she just might keep it that way. As for the spelling, she acknowledged she hadn't yet paid much attention to the spell check and grammatical suggestions programmed into the software. Her desperation lessened as her fingers worked over the keys and slowly finished off the report before sending it. Tears glazed her eyes however. She felt violated and her self-esteem diminished.

She glanced over at the clock and realized it was getting time to go to Ernest's, yet the thought of making nice pleasant talk depressed her. In the end though, it was the image of a joint of beef with all the juices that that drove her to get ready.

Clutching a most expensive wine bottle and wrapping her large woolly cardigan closer to her body for warmth against the chill of the evening air, she closed her back door behind her.

The lane at the back of the cottages was dark; the only shaft of light coming from the lamp outside the Horseshoe and the few lit-up kitchen windows that hadn't had their curtains pulled across.

Lisa pushed the Heath's normally stubborn gate hard and nearly fell through it, after finding that the hinges had been recently oiled.

'Must be Rita's doing,' she decided as she'd never seen Ernest with an oil-can in his life.

Turning the handle of the back door, she opened it, popping her head around ready to call out she'd arrived. That call however stuck in her throat as she gazed down at a body sprawled out on the floor; the head stuck under the cupboard beneath the sink.

An arm was waving at her, the voice muffled, but she got the gist of the words. She noticed a spanner a foot away from the body and passed it to the waiting hand.

A few grunts and groans later and Ernest's head appeared, his face marked with a black slime. Lisa burst out laughing. 'God man, you gave me a turn seeing your body lying there.'

He smiled and sighed; 'Even wedded bliss can have its down side you know.'

'Ever think of getting someone in?' she suggested. He looked at her in shock. 'And let Rita think I'm not capable? Oh no, never. Pass me that old towel luv, or she'll have me scrubbing the floor next.'

'Now that would be worth seeing, and I wouldn't care if I had to be a fly on the wall to witness that,' said Lisa, chuckling.

Ernest suddenly faced Lisa looking like a schoolboy who had something to confess. 'Remember I mentioned a roast beef dinner luv.' Lisa waited for the downside as Ernest stood up easing his stiffening joints and looking sheepish. 'I'm afraid it's lasagne.'

'Lasagne'! Lisa's voice raised a pitch or two, but softened as Ernest raised a finger to his lips, and tried to explain. 'Rita's idea; thought we could have dinner around the fire instead of at the table.'

'Garlic bread too, I presume,' the sarcasm in her voice barely hidden.

'Aye that's what I'm told.' He looked away and gathered up his tools; still trying to come to terms with his wife's Canadian choice of food and he not having much say in that department.

Rita came in that moment carrying a basket of washing and; ignoring Lisa, added simply. 'He fixes, and I wash and clean.'

Put like that Lisa wondered why she'd never thought of it that way herself.

'So that's what wedded bliss is all about then,' mused Lisa; 'sharing jobs and both parties quite satisfied with the arrangement.' Lisa quietly admitting that it seemed to work for them, but doubting if it would ever for her.

The lasagne turned out spicy and good; the garlic bread hot and crisp and Lisa's full-bodied red wine complementing the meal delightfully. Although, in truth, Lisa did miss her much anticipated roast beef and Yorkshire pud with all the trimmings. Relaxing afterwards, she experienced that mellow afterglow feeling of contentment. 'How's Ted?' Ernest enquired. Lisa winced and shrugged her shoulders, making it plain she didn't want to discuss him.

'And that new guy, what's his name? You know who I mean . . . Tony something or other.'

'Arbury,' stated Lisa after getting the drift of Ernest's remark and not amused; she sank back into her none communicative mode.

'Your detective constable seems nice.' Rita just couldn't let go of these obvious attempts at choosing a suitable partner for Lisa. Lisa for her part just glared back at her, wondering where all this was going.

'No match-making please,' she said. 'I'm not really in the mood, and I haven't the time.'

Rita took the hint and suggested another wine before Ernest chipped in. 'Listen luv, Rita and I are very aware that you have your back to the wall over these murders and that your mind must be going around in every direction at this very moment. Even with all my experience I keep asking myself what can the motive be; blackmail, money, power, hurt, an unstable mind or sex. All these things could lead to murder.'

Ernest's comments seemed to touch a nerve, and Lisa put her glass down and sat up; putting her head in her hands. 'I know Ernest; I've been racking my brains all day.'

'And,' he asked. He waited for a response and was visibly disappointed when none came.

Ernest suggested they take another approach; although he himself had by this time run out of fresh ideas.

Lisa sniffed, but was surprised when Rita added. 'Maybe you should move away from these suggested motives and look outside the box.' They both gazed at her with surprise and even some disbelief. Rita, realizing her naivety in these matters, reddened and went quiet.

In the distance a faint sound of a fire engine could be heard. 'Someone's got a chimney fire I guess.' muttered Ernest, glad he'd got a gas fire.

Ernest and Rita then started to reminisce about their younger years and how the roles of mothers, and even grandmothers, had changed over the years. Rita even suggested that the present youth crime rate was probably related to today's mothers going out to work and kids coming home to empty houses. Then eventually running out of conversation they all gazed at the leaping flames of the gas-fire that proved to be somewhat hypnotic.

A muffled sound of a telephone ringing brought them back to the present as they looked at each other for confirmation.

It was Lisa, who jumped up exclaiming,

'It's my mobile.' She got up and made for the kitchen were she had left her cardigan hanging on the back of a chair. She dug into the pocket, and flicked open the lid of her cell-phone. She listened for a while; stunned momentarily at what she was being told.

'Dead,' she whispered. 'Burnt alive you say, oh God what a way to go.'

Ernest was standing at the kitchen door showing little embarrassment at listening in. Lisa flicked the lid of her phone shut and stared at him. 'Someone has been found dead in a house fire.'

Ernest face paled, he had witnessed deaths from fire and it wasn't a nice experience. 'Where?' he managed to ask.

'The Ravenscroft house.'

'What about Jenny Simkins,' Rita then questioned. 'Has she been released?'

'Yes this morning,' replied Lisa, her words seemed to float from her lips without engaging her brain. 'Her lawyer said we had no grounds to keep her.' Lisa's head started to whirl and she experienced a slight dizziness. 'What if it was Jenny who started it, who would everyone blame?' Lisa knew she was a good target: A young detective sergeant, now acting detective inspector on this case with very little experience in these types of homicides.

Ernest pushed a small glass of whisky into her hand and made her drink it before adding; 'I'll phone Detective Constable Smith, and he'll come and fetch you.'

Chapter 25

A light fog had descended as Lisa stood in the doorway of number 7. Having no time to change she pulled her old cardigan closer to her chest. Hazy yellow headlights appeared ghostly as they rounded the corner of the village green. A car pulled up, Jiten leaned over opening her door.

'Oh gee,' he said, taking one look at her set features.

'Drive,' she ordered, getting in and untangling her seat belt in a flurry of frustration.

The fog got denser as they got to the main road, but ahead the sound of the fire engine was like a beacon. Nearing their destination they expected to see a huge blaze as the Ravenscroft's home was being consumed with fire. But the dark outline of the big house showed nothing but its solid structure with no hint of a fire. A few windows were lit up but they were the electric lights from within and it was plain that the house certainly was not on fire.

Jiten swept around the side of the house into the lane that led to the mill. A group of people loomed up out of the fog making him break sharply. Lisa uttered some unintelligible swear word as her head jerked forward. She flung open the car door. Suddenly she felt a sense of relief that the house was undamaged and turned to Jiten who had appeared beside her, his torch searching the area around them. The fire engine stood in the lane leading to the water towers.

'It must be around the town water towers,' said Lisa, wondering what someone was doing there in the first place. 'Best we have a word with those people as soon as possible.' She gestured to Jiten to follow her. 'I'll have a word with the fire chief as well; 'aren't those things supposed to be full of water!'

Her remark held a touch of sarcasm that her detective constable and the fire chief ignored.

Lisa made her way consciously towards the hazy lights that reflected off the fire engine, cursing herself all the way for not putting her coat on. The dark shapes of the disused water towers loomed up like a couple of medieval castle battlements.

Nothing seemed to be happening around them which left her momentarily puzzled, until she looked to her right and realised she was facing the back of the Ravencroft property and the fire engine pumps were trained on a half burnt shed.

Apart from a little damage to a few nearby trees, the shed wasn't likely to ignite anything else. 'So much for a big fire,' she mused. 'But someone had still died,' she reminded herself.

Suddenly someone called out her name. She thrust her head forward to try to identify the oddly familiar voice. The light from a hand-held torch beckoned the way, but it wasn't until she was almost upon the light holder that she recognised it was Dr. Grimshaw; the police surgeon. Apprehension gripped her stomach and the muscles of her chest tightened.

'Bad news?' she ventured, trying to keep her voice from shaking a little.

'Yes indeed; a body has been found,' he replied.

The remark held little emotion; a fact of life that Lisa had taken a long time to overcome, until she realised that it was something she had to get used to for her very survival in dealing with these nasty jobs.

His hand suddenly cupped her elbow and was leading her to where the activity was. The water pumps had stopped; the fire now out, but still smouldering. A floodlight from the fire engine lit up the area better, showing black smoke mingling with the lighter fog.

The taste of smoke and the acrid fumes filled her mouth, and she pulled her cardigan across her nose and mouth in an attempt to keep it out of her lungs.

'Here.' The police surgeon pushed a mask into her hand.

She took it gratefully and put it on. It proved a little better to breathe with, but did little to stop the tears streaming from her smoke filled eyes.

Over to her right was the obvious centre of the fire and from the look of the small area involved, realised it was the remains of the lean-to garden shed, its corrugated roof lying twisted and steaming. Black charred beams of wood and the remains of garden tools lay all around. There was nothing left.

Lisa's gaze moved quickly, having assessed the extent of damage, to where the victim lay, and right away vomit arose in her throat. She had witnessed death many times and in many forms; from stabbings, gunshots and suicides. But never had she seen the remains of someone burnt to death.

The victim still resembled a human being but only in structure, the whole of the lower and upper torso was blackened and eaten by the fire down to the bones. The obnoxious smell of burning meat hung everywhere.

A hand was placed on her shoulder. She jumped.

'Hugo Ravenscroft thinks it may be his sister.' The police surgeon spoke gently but with the professional routine of his job. 'He's in the house; better get in there lass, there's not much can be done here. All I can tell you at this moment is that it looks to be a female.'

She turned away knowing what he had said was right. Nothing could be certain about the cause of death 'til a post mortem had been completed. Occasional flashes of light turned out to be the police photographer using his skills to record the horrific night scene; but experiencing great difficulty in keeping his lenses clean.

The white coated police officers looked like ghosts as they came and went about their business, and Lisa found herself thinking of

Ted's washing for no apparent reason just as a figure loomed up by her side, startling her.

'For God's sake Jiten, don't ever do that to me again' she retorted.

He reported to her what he had found out from the bystanders. A couple using the lane that leads up to the towers first saw the blaze. They had banged on the door of the house and Mr Ravenscroft called the fire-brigade.

Lisa and Jiten started to walk through the mist and smoke towards the rest of the house.

'Light on the bloody ground man, not up in the sky.' She knocked his hand, lowering the beam. Once around the side, the house lights were fully lit.

The back door to the house was open and the odour of smoke already in the room. She closed the door behind them. The smell of coffee came as a pleasant surprise; her mouth was parched.

Hugo was sitting by the kitchen table. It was obvious he had dressed hastily, with his bare feet pushed in unlaced shoes and his unbuttoned shirt now soot marked.

The little colour he normally had seemed to have been drained away; his skin appeared white, but flecked with soot that had come from his still blackened hands.

'Did the couple see anyone around?' Lisa asked, breathing easier.

'No, but the couple did look a bit sheepish when I asked them what they were doing up the lane so late at night. However they seemed to be well aware of the seriousness of fires.'

Lisa nudged Jiten. 'Phone his doctor.' She turned to Hugo to confirm the name of his doctor. 'Potts isn't it?' she asked. He nodded, still looking in shock.

Lisa poured herself a coffee without asking and pulled up a chair before beckoning Jiten to give her his note book as he left the room.

'Was there any reason for your sister to go to the shed,' was her first question?

Hugo shook his head.

'Did your sister get any phone calls?'

He looked at her bewildered, not quite understanding where this was all leading.

'I don't know, Kristen and I had supper together and I left her reading.'

'Where did you go?' Lisa leaned forward to catch his expression as he answered.

'To bed,' he looked up at her and then, as if realising he was probably one of the suspects; he frowned, a blue vein pulsing at the side of his forehead.

'I was worn out after going over the mill's accounts. My brother-in-law left rather a mess behind before he died.' He bit his bottom lip in an effort to hold in his surging emotion. 'Kristen was fine. She said she was going to have a brandy and finish the book she was reading.' He choked a little, his voice rising. 'What the hell was she doing in the garden shed, it doesn't make sense. She had no reason to go there.'

He put his head in his hands. 'What the hell is going on, first John and now Kristen.'

"I don't know, but the only way to find out is for me to have as many answers as possible.' Lisa gave him a few minutes to compose himself before continuing.

'Did you hear her cell phone?'

'No,' he replied bluntly.

'Could you hear it from your bedroom?'

'Never thought about it, but I'd say off-hand, no. Why do you ask?'

'Just wondered if she went out to meet someone.'

'But why in the shed? why not invite who ever it was here into the house. It doesn't make any sense,' argued Hugo.

Lisa shrugged her shoulders, the thought had occurred that if she was meeting someone outside, she didn't want her brother to know about it, and secondly it was foggy and it was difficult to see. She would have taken a torch with her. She made a note to ask what was found in the rubble, before posing the question that had to be asked.

'Did your sister have any enemies or could she have been subject to blackmail?'

Hugo looked at her aghast. 'No, everyone seemed to like Kristen and I cannot think of any reason why anyone would want to blackmail her.'

'He's on his way,' said Jiten, referring to the doctor, as he re-entered the room.

Lisa indicated the detective constable sit with the victim's brother, while she went to look around the lounge.

She quickly found what she was seeking; a cell phone lying on a side table. Lisa glanced at the list of callers. There were five but no names she recognised. Still she wrote them all down and the times the calls were made.

Chapter 26

After a restless and sleep deprived night it seemed the morning couldn't be any worse for the acting Detective Inspector Pharies. However as soon as she arrived at the police headquarters she found the superintendant waiting for her in the corridor. He didn't have to say one word as his face said it all and she knew right away she was in big trouble and things could get even worse.

Like a lamb to the slaughter Lisa followed him into his office, and then waited for him to take his seat behind the desk. There was no offer of a chair for her and she was left standing awaiting the shit to hit the fan. It took but a few seconds of him staring at her with his cold eyes before Lisa's body gave an involuntary twitch as he slammed his big hand on the desk top and the full power of his voice pounded her ear drums.

'Two mistakes I will not tolerate Pharies.' he let his words sink in before continuing. 'We have another homicide on our hands as soon as we let the suspect go, what have you to say to that, might I ask?'

She reddened not from the onslaught of words, but from the tone of his voice; which proved domineering and sarcastic. In a renewed effort to boost her self esteem; she opted to defend herself.

'Sir, I'm only following the rules. The only evidence we had against Jenny Simkins was the ring. Once the former detective inspector Heath denied it was the same ring he'd seen the professor wearing, we had to let her go or we would have had the lawyers crawling all over us.'

To Lisa's surprise the chief superintendant sat back and looked deflated; his right eye twitching. Seeing him so gave her a strange sense of audacity to continue. 'The probability of coming across two sixteenth century rings with the same kind of stone is almost nil sir, but Mr Heath was absolutely positive in his identification that they were indeed two different rings.'

A long sigh was uttered from the visibly ageing man behind the desk. He cupped his large head in his hands and stared at her.

'So where's the Simkins woman now?' his voice getting louder as he started belittling her again. 'Lets hope you had the sense to keep her well under surveillance Pharies.' The threat was unmistakable.

Lisa forced herself to breath slowly; her heartbeat racing. 'She seems to be missing sir.' There was no use putting it any other way and Lisa waited for the storm to follow.

To her surprise it didn't erupt, instead the room seemed to become dead still and hardly a breath of air felt . . . . Lisa waited. A fly was crawling across his hand, and her eyes followed its every movement.

After a long interval just staring at her, he stroked his heavy shaven chin and seemed to be making up his mind. Finally he spoke. 'Find her, and bring her in by the end of the week or your career will be on the chopping block, for good this time.' The chief superintendant gave a slight wave of his hand to indicate the end of the discussion.

Thankfully she closed the door behind her and leaned against the wall feeling light-headed; her pulse racing and her heart still beating wildly. A young constable walked past her eyeing her with curiosity, then glancing at the door she had come out of; his look turned to sympathy and he walked away.

Alone with her thoughts Lisa summed up her situation and it didn't look at all good. Had she blundered that badly as soon as Jenny Simkins was released? She asked herself. Straight away there had been another homicide and this time Jenny was missing. Now deep inside she had to grapple with her belief in her own gov. and the reality of where the clues were leading. She had to face it; they all still pointed to the young frail looking woman, who looked like a scared rabbit. The decision was hard.

Her first task was to enquire how the search party for Jenny Simkins was going. The woods around her cottage were being combed and even the river scanned. Nothing up to now had established any trace of Jenny. It didn't look good.

All that remained of any signs of habitation at the cottage was a cat that had made a home in the old washhouse. It was looking well fed on mice; leaving their tails around as evidence.

Lisa's desk was littered with papers; she glanced through them finding nothing of importance just mostly routine stuff that kept the powers that be happy. She pushed her chair to and fro a couple of times till sounds of throat clearing around her, made her realise the wheels needed oiling.

Picking up the phone she dialled Dr Pott's surgery, not caring that he might be in the middle of a patient examination. However he didn't seem too upset and she quickly established that Peter was fine, and his mother had not tried to communicate with him. The only thing left to do now was to find out how the victim died and if it was indeed Kristen Tilstone. That meant waiting on the autopsy report.

The rest of the morning Lisa kept to herself, she needed to have answers for the upcoming group interaction meeting, once the autopsy report was in her hands.

Her colleagues perceived her mood following her session with chief superintendant and rightly assumed all was not well. A few kind souls offered condolences but were ignored, and they quickly realised that only Jiten was allowed into her confidence.

'Breathe deeply.' Jiten advised, after watching her shallow breathing.

She'd tried it, taking in deep complete breaths and exhaling slowly; unfortunately it only resulted in a coughing fit.

Her cell phone rang for the hundredth time it seemed, the actual figure however being only six. She lifted it to her ear and heard Tony Arbury's educated voice on the other end.

'What?'

She regretted her response almost immediately, and tried to make amends with a feeble 'sorry', but for whatever reason, he didn't seem to notice.

'Jenny Simkins,' he said quickly. 'I don't think she is capable of murder and certainly not in the way the two victims were killed.'

Lisa sighed and wondered what the hell the universities' taught these days and whether to remind him that everyone had thought that way about that "Christie Case" murderer.

Instead however she responded, 'and why not?'

'All the indications of her love for nature suggests she arbores violence.' The profiler waited for a moment, but as there was no response from Lisa, he added, 'I suggest you look for someone who isn't distressed by violence.' He waited for another response before realising there was still nothing forthcoming, and went on to say;

'Of course there is always the probability I am wrong.'

'You can bet your life on that my lad,' muttered Lisa; after closing the lid of her cell phone, thinking that the brief conversation was a total waste of time.

Yet later thinking about what he'd said, she had to admit she really couldn't see the frail Jenny cutting someone's throat. 'But then how many other murderers had looked as if they couldn't hurt a fly,' she reminded herself.

It wasn't until late afternoon that a call came from the mortuary. This is what she had been dreading, it wasn't only the body that bothered her, but the smell, the instruments and above all the still corpse ready for dissection. She'd never liked it even when she was training and always tried to stand well at the back of the class, ready to make for the door if the formalin got too strong.

But it had to be done and Lisa picked up her car-keys, telling herself it was just part of the job, like a surgeon or nurse. Then reflecting on a nursing career, she shivered. That would have been the last job in the world for her after listening to Rita's experiences.

It took longer to get to the mortuary than she'd anticipated as the traffic proved heavy for no apparent reason. However once she had turned off down a side road she had all the space in the world, apart from the meat wagon as the locals called it.

An ambulance stood with its doors open by the double gates at the front of the mortuary which many years ago had been a workhouse. Lisa sat awhile in the small car park watching the attendants transferring a body to its new home. They seemed to be laughing at something the male mortuary attendant had said. Lisa wondered if her mother had suffered the same indignities, then reflected on herself sharing a joke or two over a corpse. Probably keeps one sane she thought, forgiving them as she opened the door.

The passageway to the autopsy room was narrow; white gleaming walls and a well scrubbed tiled floor. Her footsteps echoed over the tiles underfoot. A slight drift of formaldehyde hit her full force, she stopped holding her breath, but when that didn't work she took out her handkerchief and held it to her nose. Suddenly the half glazed doors of the pathology lab were before her, and it took all her strength to push it open.

A young attractive blonde holding a tray of instruments greeted her.

'Detective Pharies?'

Lisa nodded not wanting to look around and yet pulled in by a curiosity she couldn't resist.

There it was centre stage, the green plastic covered body of a once young and healthy woman, laid out for its final indignity. The stainless steel table shone from its cleanliness, and the instruments set out with precision on a tray with the stainless kidney bowls awaiting the organs.

Someone was moving behind her. Lisa whipped around to find the same attractive woman holding a gown and mask.

Lisa put them on letting the woman tie the gown and hand her a paper mask. This is what a surgeon must feel like thought Lisa, suddenly feeling trussed up like a turkey. Next came the rubber gloves, but she had already made a firm vow to herself not to touch anything; gloves or not.

For what seemed a lifetime, but was in fact barely two minutes, Lisa tried to avert her eyes from the remains of the corpse on the table and was seriously thinking of leaving, when the double doors were flung open and in walked the home office pathologist, already dressed for dissection.

He nodded; picked up a folder of notes, spent a few moments glancing over them, then moved to the table.

The blonde handed him gloves and tied a mask around his face. He pulled away the sheet covering the body, and it was at that precise moment Lisa fainted.

Coming back from the blackness seemed a long journey, and when at last she focussed, it was Jiten's face that hovered about her. She was sitting on a chair outside the autopsy room.

Seeing the colour coming back into her face, Jiten grinned but knew better than comment. They sat alone for what seemed like hours, but was, in truth only one hour by her watch, when the pathologist came out pulling down his mask. He smiled, giving her a mischievous boyish look she hadn't expected.

'Okay?'

She nodded.

'Happens a lot,'

He pulled up a chair; too close for comfort, as he still smelt of the same sickly fumes that nauseated her.

'I'll have the report on your desk by tomorrow,' he said. 'But the gist of it is that the cause of death was not from burning but from strangulation.'

For a moment he looked with concern at Lisa white face, but went on. 'There was damage to the thyroid bone.' He pointed to his own throat. 'It's located just above the larynx.'

Lisa stared at him. 'Are you are sure she'd been strangled?'

'Put my reputation on it. My guess is she was strangled in the shed and whoever did it then set fire to it.'

Jiten then asked his one and only question.

'Would the person who strangled her have to be strong?'

'Not in this case, the victim was strangled from behind, and would have been taken off-guard. Once the rope was around the neck, it just had to be tightened.'

'Rope?' voiced Lisa.

'Oh yes, even after burning the path lab found marks and fibres. It certainly was a rope.'

'How can you indentify the victim for certain.' asked Lisa, inquisitively?

'We have her wedding ring with an inscription on it.' he answered in a matter-of-fact voice. 'I think that's evidence enough.'

Chapter 27

'I'm worried about that girl.' Rita stepped back from the front room window letting the curtains fall back into place after watching Lisa's car pass the house.

'Um.' her husband responded half heartedly staring at the local newspaper and carrying on sipping his tea, whilst at the same time the pencil that lay between his fingers tapped on the leather arm of his chair.

Rita slipped a magazine under his paper and pencil and sighed. Since Ernest had discovered the game of Sudoku, live conversation had become a series of grunts. She took one last look at him before entering the kitchen, a little smile hovering on her lips. She understood that her Ernest would always need something to solve, even if the end result was just self-satisfaction.

She ignored the plastic gloves by the sink, having bought them with all good intentions of caring for her skin. Instead she lowered her hands into the hot soapy water and began washing up.

A ray of sunlight played across her face as she lifted it up towards the sun. Suddenly the full peel of the church bells of St Anne's swung into action and rang out loudly calling the faithful to Sunday prayer as it had always done over the centuries.

Rita's hands stopped washing and lay limp in the soft suds as she looked over to where the sounds of the bells came from. All she could see was the end of the stone wall that marked the church yard and the tip of one of the ancient grave monuments. It was a comforting thought to the village, that it was looked over by the beautiful church structure of St Anne's

Someone had told her that part of the church building dated back to Saxon times, and that it had once been Roman Catholic before the Reformation. She smiled remembering her teacher telling the class that Danesbury survived by knowing which side to be on during those turbulent times of the Civil War. Rita had decided long ago that the town's folk couldn't have been that religious as they once sold the town's bible to replace a dead bear that was kept for baiting. Needs must, she supposed bear baiting was just as important to them as well as caring for their souls.

Her own religious views had changed dramatically over the years. Being a midwife had left any notion of a miraculous virgin birth in fairyland with her childhood. However there had been times when she had witnessed great grief and the belief in an afterlife seemed the only way for many to carry on. She was sure there was no holy mystery about religions, and evolution was just as wonderful in so many ways. However her childhood education in the church school held many memories, for the most part good; even if it was only another form of brain washing. Although Ernest might differ on that point as the vicar was pretty handy at flinging books towards those pupils, not paying attention during his catechism classes.

However Rita still loved the architecture of the old churches, especially St. Anne's with all its ancient history. It was at the very centre of the village and was the mother church of the surrounding towns. Within its walls it held records ancestral buffs would have given their right arm for.

She suddenly had a nostalgic feeling she would like to go to the morning service. She liked the new rector; he was a bit more realistic than some had been before him and local gossip could be exchanged later on over coffee. She dried her hands quickly as the sun was filling the room and lifting her spirits.

'Ernest.' she called, popping her head around the door, but after a moment of waiting for some reply, she gave up trying to get his attention. The pencil was still working over the paper, and he was in his own world of figures and square boxes

Her sudden enthusiasm for a morning out however quickly waned as the sun now sought seeking the cover of nearby clouds and her thoughts now centred on the joint of beef in the fridge.

Ernest's intense concentration broke shortly after. He put his paper down, laying the pencil on top of it, staring for a moment at the magazine underneath it and wondering how it got there. Changing his point of focus, he slid back in his chair and gazed at the blank ceiling noticing a slight crack in it. Lisa's face and Rita's concern over her came to mind for no apparent reason.

'Yes I do worry about Lisa,' he admitted to himself. The lass looked at the end of her tether and he knew the feeling well, having been there himself in the past over a couple of difficult cases.

He screwed up his eyes. The thin crack in the ceiling wasn't a crack after all; it was the tiny thread of a spider's web. It hung motionless, but held his attention as he sucked at his bottom lip; deep in thought.

The small thread waved in a draft of air. It reminded him to concentrate on the small things that may seem insignificant. He sighed, wondering if Lisa might give up and he knew she would never forgive herself if she did. He needed to think.

'Cuppa?' This time he heard his wife's voice and answered to the affirmative before going back to his self-interrogation. The front lobe of his brain was already receiving a fresh blood supply, as he tried to estimate the number of flies that could be drawn into this latest and developing web of murder.

He mentally reviewed everyone that could have had something to do with the deaths.

'Jenny Simkins.' The same past questioning came up but with no fresh insights. She appeared gentle, loved the country life and her cottage. Good mother by all accounts. 'So what could trigger aggression?' he mused; 'maybe relocation perhaps.'

Ernest racked his brains about her but couldn't come up with anything other than her being a possible psychopath, but there was no evidence of that kind of mental disturbance in her past.

'Hugo Ravenscroft?' Ernest thought hard. 'Nothing suspicious in his past; good boss, wasn't a womanizer and difficult to imagine him murdering his own sister.'

Ernest let his imagination run wild. It had served him well on a few occasions; looking outside the box as he called it.

'Was Hugo gay?' He had never married and wondered if Hugo had ever attended Oxford University?

Then there had been that phone call to the Ravenscroft's from the Saxon Arms. What was that all about?' Ernest chewed on his bottom lip harder.

'No evidence there.'

'What about Dr. Potts?' he considered. 'What did they really know of him? Had Lisa looked at his past records as a doctor elsewhere?' 'Why was he insisting on looking after Peter?'

His last thought he didn't like, and it made him even more determined to get Lisa to check up on the doctor's past.

'Why was John Tilstone killed? and what did he know that was important, again was it about Hugo's possible sexual orientation, if any?'

Rita came in with his tea, took one look at his rigid and unchanging stare and went back to defrosting the beef in the kitchen. She well knew that look, and would find out later what he'd come up with as she left him to it.

Ernest's head began to ache and realised he was getting paranoid. Then after taking his time sipping his tea, he leaned over the arm of his chair, fiddled under the side of it and eventually bringing out a folded piece of paper.

He unfolded it staring at a faded map. It was a copy of the one he had obtained from the town's archives and it gave details of the land around the mill in the early middle 1600's.

Peering at it closely for a while, he rubbed his eyes, put the map down, got up and picked his reading glasses from the mantelpiece. Putting them on, he picked up the map again and went over to the table by the window.

He pushed the newly opened daffodil bulbs to one side, ignoring the trail of light soil that escaped.

Ernest spread out the copy of the map on the table for a closer inspection using the better light from the window. Only part of the writing was identifiable with some parts faded and it took a while to realise that part was in Latin and part in old English.

It was a hand drawn map identifying land ownership with the boundaries marked by a series of small dashes. A river was recognisable; its twists and turns marked well, even the woods and copses were well defined. Ernest looked closer and was surprised to find the river identified as the river Congo and for a second wondered if he had the right one after all. He bit his pencil frowning after studying it a while longer before calling for Rita.

She came rubbing her hands on her apron and asking what it was all about. He explained his dilemma, asking his question.

'Had our river always been called the Dane?'

Rita giggled and pushed her elbow into his ribs. 'Oh Ernest, you never did listen in class. Too busy polishing your conkers, I suppose.'

He snorted and thought it not a very good idea for Rita to express his trophy conkers in such a way; people might not understand about conker fights.

'The Danes; invaded remember?' She looked at him pitifully. History had come and gone with Ernest. 'Now what are you studying?' asked Rita.

Church forgotten, Sudoku forgotten. Even the joint of beef was still left uncooked as Ernest and Rita poured over the copy of the old town map from the 1600's.

Chapter 28

Her head felt like a ton weight as Lisa raised it from the pillow. The constant throbbing in her temples caused a slight nauseating effect. Gingerly easing herself to sitting position, she caught sight of herself in the dressing table mirror which made her feel a good deal more wretched.

Coffee and lots of it was the only thing she could focus on and maybe aspirin. She felt like hell, and it was only on eventually reaching the kitchen that she came face to face with the reason.

A quarter-full bottle of pure malt whisky and its companion, an empty glass, stood on the table. It was all the evidence she needed to know. She had gone to bed in no good state and mentally wondered how she had managed the steep stairs. It was a scary thought.

The pounding in her head reminded her of her desperate attempt to shut out the feeling of failure, in the only job she'd ever wanted. She gave a little sarcastic laugh; the bloody whisky having done nothing and it tasted awful as well.

She tried to stop her hand from shaking as she plugged in the kettle.

Once boiled, the coffee did help a little although in truth she knew it was more the three aspirins she'd taken with it.

'What now?' she mused, as she gazed over the rim of her coffee mug to stare absentmindedly at the window. It was grey outside; the grey feeling she felt. Not a sound either. Sunday in Gelsby didn't start until the first soundsof St. Anne's bells and that was enough to waken even the dead in the graveyard.

Her mother always said Sunday was family time and her dad had always insisted it was a day of rest, with a visit to the pub, before lunch maybe. Lisa found herself smiling; rest for her dad maybe, but her mother was always expected to come up with that extra special Sunday dinner. She gave a wisp of a smile remembering it seemed to work for them, just as she knew Ernest and Lisa would be sharing tales and intimacies over a cooked breakfast, Rita doing the washing up, while Ernest would put his feet up.

She swirled the remaining coffee around her cup watching a brown stains appear. There wasn't much she could do today. Most of the police force would be off duty wherever possible and the headquarters half empty; the remaining souls generally marking time and keeping their desks tidy without straining too hard. Trouble was she couldn't come up with anything that would move things forward, apart from extending the search area for the Simkins girl and re-interviewing people.

'Ernest has been no bloody good either.' The angry thought popped up out of nowhere and she immediately felt ashamed. It was not his patch any longer but hers.

Getting up, she opened the fridge, her stomach immediately objected strongly and she closed it again, resting her back against the cool door and thinking.

'I was a little unfair to Ted about life on the farm the last time I was there; maybe I should give it another try and be more positive. Hell, anything has to be better than this.' The "this" she was referring to was the bottle of golden liquid on the table that had caused her headache and unsettled stomach in the first place.

Half an hour later as her car passed the Heath house, she could have sworn she saw more net-curtains moving. A little cynical smile played on her lips at the thought of Rita taking up the age old village practice of keeping a check on the comings-and-goings of Gelsby's inhabitants.

Suddenly her head seemed to explode as the St. Anne's bells peeled out over the village calling the faithful to Holy Communion. The noise stayed with her all the way to Ted's farm. As she turned into the farm's drive, she was confronted by the sign on the farm gate. Please Keep Gate Closed. She held back a forthcoming curse as she realised she had to get out of the car to open the farm gate, get in again, drive through and then out again to close it.

The fields either side however looked every bit the green pasture lands of old paintings, and for once Lisa felt pride in the Cheshire countryside. She opened her window, and slowed down as she heard the soft call of a morning dove together with the low sound of a cow mooing, followed by the sharp bark of a dog. All country normal sounds, yet she'd not really noticed them before.

Her brief moments of contemplation were usually shattered by the sound of her mobile; instinctively her hand went to the outside of her jacket pocket checking to make sure she had her mobile with her.

Nearing the old farm house, she made a quick decision to park at the front and not at the back where last time she found herself almost ankle deep in cow dung, and that pong which took such a long time to get rid of. It had remained with her after her last visit, for most of her journey back home.

The front door opened before she had even turned off the key of her car. The girl called Susan stood there eyeing her suspiciously and Lisa found herself expecting the girl to ask why she'd come.

'Ted around?' She tried to sound as if her being there was a day-to-day occurrence.

Susan looked at her as if she was an imbecile, before adding in a manner what should have been obvious to anyone.

'He's with the cows.' Her tone gave Lisa the feeling the girl was sneering at her in her own way.

Lisa felt the heat rising up to her face. After all these months in a relationship with Ted, she should have at least known the times of the day that were the most important to him. She should have made an effort to understand his working day better. Lisa stared at the girl, who seemed to know her boyfriend better than herself. She heard herself replying, 'I know that; just want to know where the cows are?'

An expression of disbelief in the matters of farming slid over Susan's face. 'In the cowshed of course,' pointing to the only structure around that could have been used for that purpose. Lisa turned away, pretending to look into her car. After considering the very real possibility of getting cow dung over her shoes again, she made her decision quickly and got out slamming the car door behind her, then pushing past the girl; she entered the house. 'I'll wait for him here.'

Susan shrugged her shoulders and went over to the kitchen table and a large mixing bowl, then without even a glance at her visitor; started to stir it. Something else also started to stir in the corner of the large kitchen. A black and white collie lifted its head and stared at Lisa before lowering it onto its paws; keeping one open eye on her.

Lisa sat on an old fashioned wooden arm chair watching Susan hand-mixing. Her ginger hair looked longer than last time and the freckles not as visible. She's quite pretty, thought Lisa; experiencing a little flash of jealousy.

The door from the outside opened and Lisa arose to greet Ted but instead found herself facing Susan's father; the old man she'd talked to last time she visited. He looked at her with surprise, took off his tatty cap and greeted her with just two words.

'Nice day?'

He then proceeded to look into a black pot on the range. Lisa guessed it was a stew from the aroma. Satisfied he was going to eat; he drew up a chair and faced the newcomer.

'Thar's well?'

She nodded, thinking sarcastically he was a man of very few words, namely two. However he surprised her by telling his daughter to get the kettle on for the young lady.

Lisa's face brightened a little, it was a long time since anyone had made her feel special; even though the response from his daughter was merely a sniff.

'So lass, I see from the papers things are not going too well for the likes of you.'

Lisa looked up defensively, and then realised there was no malice in his question, just interest. Susan handed her a steaming mug of strong tea.

'Biscuits' ordered her dad and got another glare from his daughter in return.

The biscuits were homemade and delicious which made Lisa's spirits drop a little as the old man carried on talking, while the crumbs spilled down his dirty sweater.

'Cows are the only thing that keeps this farm going these days. Not like having your own land. Can't even sell it off and be done with it.' He stopped short. 'Take this land here, although it's been in the Green family for generations; it could never be their own, yet they are the ones that have worked themselves to the bone on it.'

Lisa was aware Susan was listening; the sound of the spoon now hitting the sides of the bowl with vigour.

'Why didn't they ever buy the land?' asked Lisa, her interest was in all honesty, about the past Green families and not Ted's prospects.

'Nay lass, it isn't about money.' His voice lowered. 'It's because its glebe land.'

Lisa thought back to her church school days for a moment; and those Friday mornings when the rector often told them about the long history of St. Anne's.

'You mean the church owns it.'

He nodded. 'This here is glebe land and poor it is and always was; too near to the marsh you see.'

Lisa was aware the marsh was every parent's nightmare and a warning sign to its dangers had recently been put up for anyone walking that way.

'The Green's once owned the land down by the mill.' He inclined his head westward and Lisa guessed it was the Ravencroft mill he was talking about.

'Near the Ravenscroft's land?' asked Lisa with interest, realizing how many old farming families truly belonged to this area of Cheshire.

'Aye, taken from them in the past; the church now lets them work the glebe land.' He smiled a secret smile; 'dare say the church always made money, having good farmers to plough its land.'

The dog barked, stretched its legs and walked over stiffly to greet Ted who had come in. He stared in astonishment at Lisa, then took of his cap and came over to kiss her cheek, she tried not to flinch; the smell somewhat overpowering and followed by a wince from Susan at the kitchen table.

Lisa stayed for the best part of two hours, all the time conscious that everyone around her only really wanted to get on with their daily routine.

It had been raining during her visit and on leaving; Lisa found the farm drive harder to manoeuvre her car. She was glad to eventually close the farm gate behind her.

Chapter 29

The sun never emerged again after its first morning rays had managed to pierce the gathering clouds for a short time.

Nor did the possibility of rain come to anything apart from a few scattered rain drops. In fact it proved to be a typical English day and life in the village carried on as normal.

The only abnormal occurrence was the fact that Rita managed to persuade Ernest to get out of his chair and go for a long walk. The distance wasn't discussed beforehand but soon Ernest realised he was being led to the lane that was quite a hike as it rounded the marsh and church lands.

At first he was aware of the cold damp creeping into his bones and the stiffness of his back and legs, but as they strolled and Rita chatted, he felt quite good, and even felt springiness to his stride.

They chatted about Canada, their youth and news topics, both deliberately skirting the one thing on both their minds; 'Lisa!' . . . . each knowing full well they would eventually get around to it.

A kingfisher flew out of the reeds obviously disturbed, the smell of the marsh land hung; not unpleasant but fragrant with mosses and vegetation. Celandines and soldier buttons spread out making yellow and orange carpets, tempting any passer by to come and view, while Nelly Longarms waited patiently in the dark water and mud.

The signs to warn the public about the dangers of straying from the path were well placed, as many a child had been taken by the marsh over the years.

Soon the couple came to the edge of the marshy land and fields spread out before them. In the distance clumps of trees stood on the mounds of ground and watching over it all, The Cloud; a mountain that marked the southern end of the long mountainous back bone of England called the Pennine Chain, which loomed up on the skyline.

Along the edge of the field they walked single file along a centuries old track, but as it broadened, Rita slipped her hand into Ernest's. He gave it a little squeeze and smiled at her.

He was glad he'd come, the timeless pathways seem to bring the past into one continuous stream of events, leading to the present moment. His mind cleared, even his stride had gathered length and had a spring in it.

Ahead of them in the distance loomed the back of St. Anne's and the wall of the old churchyard. Facing them, the path forked giving them two alternatives to reach the centre of the village again. One was to carry on walking until they met the main road, a detour which would eventually bring them back to the village, the other, more of a shortcut really which would bring them directly to the church with the added incentive of a long drink at the Horseshoe.

It only took a quick glance at each other and the decision was made, both heading for the stone wall that encircled the old graveyard and church. It seemed the same decision had been made many times before by many people as a portion of the wall had toppled giving access to the churchyard itself. A few pieces of paper and a couple of plastic cups lay forlornly against the toppled stones. Shaking her head at the litter, Rita gathered it up and climbed through the gap into the churchyard where she deposited it into a wire basket near a mound of decaying flowers and grass.

She turned wiping her hands together in a gesture as if to clean them. Ernest was standing a little way off; his back towards her; legs apart and hands clasped behind his back. Without turning he called her over to an old gravestone.

Rita looked at the leaning grave stone; now partly moss covered and could just make out the carved lettering on it.

"Seth Potts 15 . . . . something"; the weather having badly eroded the rest of it

Rita knew what her husband was thinking.

'I suppose it could be an ancestor of our Dr Potts, although it doesn't seem he had a wife or offspring, there's only his name.'

Ernest sucked at his bottom lip. 'It does tell us the family was buried here though.' Ernest considered his options; make for the Horseshoe and call it a day, or to further stimulate his brain cells to find out if the church still held old records.

Rita must have picked up his thoughts for when she happened to see a figure of a clergyman coming towards them; it seemed a good opportunity to at least investigate the possibility of further research.

For a brief moment Ernest stared in confusion at the short plump figure weaving his way around the old tombs and flagstones. Then he remembered that their rector had been replaced temporarily by another recently.

Rita stepped forward; her hand outstretched.

'Welcome to Gelsby, Don Phillips isn't it?'

The two clasped hands which were shaken vigorously. Ernest sighed, he was forever amazed at her knowledge of the coming and goings around the village; yet at the same time felt a glow of pride.

What amazed Ernest more was the easy way his plans were not thwarted as the temporary rector was only too pleased to allow them to look through the archives of the church's books and records. The rector himself was all for having this information made freely available by having it downloaded to computer files for everyone's interest.

'Ancestry is a big thing at the moment,' he remarked, happily dusting down boxes with the dates Ernest and Rita needed. Thoroughly enjoying the interest shown; the reverend Phillips even brought in a tray of coffee. 'Sorry no biscuits left,' he added, his face colouring a little as he patted his stomach

It was interesting work ploughing through names that were familiar to Ernest and Rita; names of the ancestors of many people in the village still bearing the same names and never moving from the area.

Keeping their focus on the job in hand, Ernest and Rita were rewarded at last. The name Potts was found and the associated births—marriages and deaths together with witnesses were traced back through the generations and it proved to be extremely interesting.

The marriage of John Potts to Martha Bond was witnessed by E. Simkins on July 4th 1642. However within a year, John Potts seemed to have died of "wasting disease".

'Probably TB,' suggested the rector; sipping his coffee and peering at them with his bright blue eyes over the rim of his cup. 'Ancestors of yours are they?'

They didn't have to answer as a call came from the top of the stairs. The rector shrugged his shoulders as if the weight of the world lay on them and disappeared. Ernest leaned back against the cold stone wall of the church archives thinking, before adding; 'Rita, I think our Dr. Potts family and the Simkins family share the same past.'

Rita nodded somewhat absent-mindedly as she was thumbing through dates with the intention of proving once and for all that Jenny's great grandparents were indeed married but after a fruitless search, she came to the conclusion that the family rumour of unwedded females was true, for all the children born to Jenny's great grandmother had her maiden name. Still Rita harboured an admiration for the woman who had given birth five times and knew how hard it would have been. The thought the man she was involved with must have already been married also crossed her mind.

Rita's mind suddenly clicked as she remembered something. 'Ernest, remember that notebook the librarian at Oxford said the professor had left behind and which he gave to you. Do you still have it, or did you pass it on to Lisa?'

Ernest stared at her, and then flushed as he quickly straightened up. He remembered being given the notebook. It was no more than four by three inches with a soft black cover. He frantically searched the pockets of the jacket he was wearing only to find the lining of one of the pockets damaged. However the notebook was fortunately still lying in the bottom of the jacket's inner lining.

Retrieving it, he fingered through it. Stopping at a page he squinted at the small writing in the half light of the room. He sucked in his breath as the word Potts could just about be made out. Ernest's hand trembled slightly and his voice wavered. 'Rita, I think we have something here.'

'What?' she almost stumbled to his side and gazed at what seemed to be a family chart, but it was what preceded it that was the surprise.

The writing was the professor's, and there was no mistaking his hand writing. What he'd written had been written in a hurry, as if he'd copied it from somewhere.

It read that when Elizabeth (Beth Simkins) was declared a witch, her nurse and maid had disappeared with the Simkins young son called John and, fearing for his future had changed his name to Potts.

Underneath this writing there was a sketchy chart.

John Potts m Anne Clayton

1665—Twins, Simeon and Jules.

* Simeon Potts carries on with the name Potts; Jules reverts to his real name Simkins.

A star highlighted the rushed handwriting, on the page. Neither Rita nor Ernest spoke for a while, letting the information sink in. Then Rita rushed over to the boxes searching for the late 1600's-early 1700's information and looked for the name Simkins. After an intense search she came up triumphant, putting an old parchment page in front of Ernest's eyes.

Jules Simkins: Births, Marriages and Deaths.

They poured over each generation until they came up to Sara Simkins, unmarried with a daughter Jenny.

Ernest and Rita faced each other across the table each with the same thought. At last, it was Rita who ventured the telling of it.

'Do you think Dr. Potts knows of his relationship to Jenny?'

Ernest's eyes moved to the papers, and then back to meet Rita's enquiring expression again, before adding. 'He was keen to look after Peter. Based on the fact he's into ancestry and history, I would hazard a guess at yes, he most certainly does; so the question now becomes. What had he got to gain from not mentioning it?'

'Well it can't be the land after all the centuries that have passed.' Rita continuing her line of thought, before adding, 'maybe as a doctor he just doesn't want to be associated with Jenny, after all many people see her as a simpleton.'

Ernest noticed Rita blushing, the last statement wasn't her style, but he recognised the truth for what it was worth. Suddenly Rita slapped the top of the table with her bare hand, a shower of dust floated up.

'The toadstone ring,' she almost croaked getting it out.

Ernest stared at her at first, it sounded daft, but the more he thought, the more he realised the toadstone ring was always involved, from the professor's to Jenny's and then the professor's ring disappearing mysteriously when he was murdered.

'Why? What was its importance?' Ernest muttered.

A cheerful voice asking if they had researched all their needs, brought them to the present and, after handshakes and thank-you's and a somewhat feeble promise by Rita that they would be in church on Sunday; they left.

'Drink luv?' asked Rita as they neared the Horseshoe. He nodded; all in all it had been a most satisfactory day and he was about to enjoy its reward with a long cool beer and pie.

Chapter 30

Ernest drove past the red brick wall that separated the pavement from Dr. Pott's property. He noted the wrought iron gates and brass plaque, and was aware of the same feeling of intimidation he had experienced as a child.

True the wall and the gates didn't appear so high now as they did then and the house itself looked somewhat smaller. Only the trees had actually gained in width and height. Memories of scrambling up the wall to get at the best conker tree for miles around came back. Sadly the last doctor had had it cut down.

Memories also of sitting in the cold surgery room built around the side of the house for the National Health patients did nothing to boost his confidence. All his childhood memories were of his hidden fear of examinations, needles, stitches and that dreadful stuff he'd had plastered on his head at times to control head lice.

The other childhood fear was of the doctor ever finding out that he was lying when asking for a note to stay off school at exam time.

After cruising around the narrow streets in his car Ernest had talked himself back into the present and adulthood with all its responsibilities.

Once parked, the old familiar habit of being the one in charge of interviewing, overcame all is childhood sense of inferiority. Ernest had phoned beforehand and the doctor had remembered chatting with him some time back and even remembered Ernest's former profession and that he now lived near to the young lady detective. Ernest, explaining he needed to talk to him about some ancestry that might be of interest to him. The doctor went quiet for awhile, before saying he would find space in his busy schedule.

It was the doctor himself that answered the door, leading Ernest him down a passageway that smelt of regular polishing on its dark oak floors.

He was shown into the same room that Lisa had been in but this time it wasn't coffee that was offered but a glass of Glenfiddich. A bit early in the day for Ernest but he didn't refuse it, thinking there were some compensations for being retired after all.

Jeremiah Potts sat back in a large leather chair, crossing his legs and cupping his glass tightly. He peered at Ernest with the same expression he used when assessing patients for physical and mental flaws.

At last he spoke.

'So Ernest, what's this all about?' He eyed his companion with interest. 'You mentioned you had some information on the name of Potts.'

Ernest nodded and took a sip of the excellent whisky, letting it warm the back of his throat.

The doctor leaned back and grinned. 'There are lots of potty people around.'

It was an old joke from Ernest's school days and he let it go. He put his glass down on the table beside him, and leaned forward, legs spread apart and hands clasped together. He gazed at his host for a few moments before breaking the frailty of the conversation that he had tried to cover up with too much friendliness. Ernest made eye contact and held it. 'I believe you come from London. Am I right?'

The doctor nodded.

But Ernest hadn't finished and he came back sharply. 'But your ancestors come from around these parts don't they.' It was a statement, not a question.

The doctor flinched and looked at him with surprise and nodded. Ernest however gave him no space to talk, as he continued and about to play his ace card.

'Your ancestors were Simkins originally weren't they?' he stopped for a second watching the doctor's reaction. It came in the form of his hand shaking, nearly spilling the whisky. Ernest knew he had scored, but the apple cart needed tipping a little further to send the apples rolling.

However he was disappointed, instead of some further reaction, none came, just a sigh from the doctor, then . . . . 'Yes you are right and congratulations on your research.' He looked at Ernest with genuine respect. 'But tell me, how did you find that out?' He seemed genuinely interested.

'I have my means.' It was all Ernest was willing to offer, he leaned back and let the fiery liquid slip down his throat, then glanced at the bottle's label to be etched into his mind for future reference.

Potts followed his gaze. 'Another?' he offered, but let it go, when Ernest shook his head reluctantly. It wouldn't do to damage his repetition if stopped whilst driving.

The doctor was again speaking. 'I suppose you really want know why I never mentioned that Jenny Simkins was from the same family tree so to speak.'

Ernest nodded.

'Would you, in my position?'

The blank look that the doctor received back drew colour to his face, and Ernest realised the doctor was genuinely embarrassed. Jenny was a character known for being a little off-base as it were.

The doctor poured himself a half glass and swirled it around in the glass before he spoke again.

'Years ago, at med school in fact, I got interested in ancestry, that so many people were doing at the time. I grew up in London, but remembered my grandparents came from Cheshire and also their parents before that. Potts is a common name and easy to trace so I started on the computer which was just becoming available to many. Then I got to examining Record Office information.'

He stopped and smiled. The name Potts by the way means the family probably started off by making clay pots and things.'

He got no reaction. 'I digress, sorry.'

Ernest nodded, but not before he'd let his own imagination wander. Heath probably came from the common land on the outskirts of most towns where once gibbets were erected to hang criminals when required. He shuddered as if someone had walked over his grave.

The doctor was talking again. 'Finding nothing more in the Record Offices before the eighteen hundreds I searched church records in Cheshire. 'I eventually found two brothers called Potts, although one later had changed his name to Simkins. Not knowing the reason why one was Potts and the other Simkins, I followed the Simkins line back to a Beth Simkins. Beth had a nurse, and it was she who brought up Beth's child after Beth's untimely death. Her name was Martha Potts.'

Ernest nodded, confirming that he knew all this and there was a suppressed respect for him in the doctor's eyes.

'I did find something out that held my interest and still does for that matter. It was the legend about a toadstone ring that Beth Simkins was supposed to have passed on to her nurse.'

Ernest's ears picked up as the doctor continued.

'Peter told me his mother had a very old ring she kept in a recess in the wall behind the dresser, and had seen his mother move the dresser and take a box out of it.'

At first Ernest thought that this was all the doctor was going to impart; but he went on to tell all.

'Our family always knew about the toadstone you see and the story that was passed down was that it held some value, but it was never taken seriously, till Peter mentioned Jenny had it and I became curious.'

Ernest whistled; things were now beginning to make some sense after all. 'Any idea what?' he asked, his interest and energy fully returning to the investigation in hand. The doctor looked embarrassed, fiddling with his glass and avoiding eye contact before adding. 'No idea.'

He then took a moment before deciding to continue. 'I know this sounds bad but things change and people do too. I admit I was very interested in the toadstone ring, believing I had every right to its secrets.

Even if I'm known by the name Potts; Simkins is my blood line. I once asked Jenny about it and she became very aggressive and said it was none of my business.'

The doctor looked shameful. 'I couldn't even bring myself to let her know I was just as much a Simkins as she was, and I let it go. Then when all this business came up with the professor . . . . , what's his name?, being murdered and Jenny being accused, I saw a way of getting closer to whatever other secrets her cottage would hold through looking after Peter.'

When he had finished, the doctor sat with his head in his hands, awaiting a tirade of disgust from Ernest. And after a while, when nothing was forthcoming, he sat up.

'So now you know my guilty secret.' He seemed to have shrunk, his face pale and his pale eyes holding a look of a timid dog about to be chastised.

'Well that's it I suppose.' said Ernest quietly, before wondering where all this wealth information was taking him anyway.

'One thing Ernest,' the doctor had got up and was pouring himself another measure. 'I have grown to generally like the boy and will do everything in my power to give him some stability in his life.' His lips curled as if mocking. 'After all, we are family aren't we?'

Ernest was about to get up when the doctor faced him again; this time from a standing position and looking down at him.

'Peter says that there is a recess in the wall behind the dresser where his mother keeps things.' He waited for Ernest to say something, and when nothing came, he added.

'Fancy a look, I can cancel surgery just this once.'

Ernest nodded. 'My car or yours?'

Chapter 31

The police headquarters was busy as all Mondays were. Voices were loud and the chatter constant, which usually related to the weekend's highlights and activities. The ones that had been called in over the weekend complained and as usual the married men moaned about their partner's lack of understanding. Lisa wondered if the other half knew that the extra work load usually meant a call at the pub on the way home. No doubt it was called a conference if late returning home. She knew; she'd been there.

Sally Booth, the newest and brightest in Lisa's estimation and the prettiest in male's opinion popped her head over the screen partitioning Lisa's space.

'Mr Heath called; something to do with land ownership.'

Lisa nodded but made no attempt to put a stop to the rumours that would no doubt fly around the office that she was in the process of buying land. Let them think what they liked, at least she would go up a notch

She shuffled through the general boring stuff and decided to concentrate on the most important. She filled in her work sheet hours with one overriding thought that she may need every penny in future.

Tracking through the stack of e-mails on the computer, none proved of great importance, so she sat back pushing the office chair gliding on its wheels backwards. 'Ouch.'

She wheeled around full circle to find Jiten holding up his size twelve and rubbing his foot.

'Sorry.'

'Ok.'

The two simple words left them staring at one another; each hoping for some bright idea to explode. Nothing did.

'Coffee?' Jiten asked, picking up on the depressed mood of his boss.

It took a couple of moments to think about it before her stomach rejected the suggestion.

'No thanks.'

At that Jiten felt deflated and leaned against the office partition that threatened to move an inch or two. A grunt from the other side warning whoever it was, he was not relinquishing even the smallest amount of space.

'So we are nowhere nearer to solving this one then.' the tiredness in Jiten's voice reflected a bad night's sleep.

Lisa analysed him for a while before swinging her chair around to face her computer, staring at it momentarily before getting up.

'Check whether John Tilstone had any debts worth worrying about. There must be something we've missed, . . . and oh Jiten,' she called as he turned to go. 'I want that report about the mill's finances on my table today, understand?'

He winced at the tone of her voice and decided it would take more than one cup of coffee to bring him out of his sleep deprived state.

Her mobile rang; it was the chief superintendant's number. She stared at it of a few moments then quickly pocketed it. Reprimand for sure; but she had to get out of the building and have space to think.

Once in the car she just sat; hands gripping the steering wheel and looking into space. 'Guess this is what is known as drawing a blank' she told herself and, noting the feeling of laughter that wanted to follow. She took a deep breath, allowing her fingers to lessen their hold; before reflecting on the burnt body that had once being a vital person.

'She must have been meeting someone.' Lisa racked her brains, 'but who?' There were no calls on Kristin's mobile and the house phone didn't have a call display. All she could do was to await the phone company's list of calls to the house. She had an uneasy feeling it would be local, and from a phone box.

Without analyzing why, she knew she had to go back to the area of the homicide and have another look around. Ernest would call it a hunch, and would have advised her to follow it up. She engaged the gears and put her foot down, making for Ravens Nest.

Instead of using the front entrance, Lisa retraced her steps on the night of the fire.

She parked her car on the opposite side of the road and made for the gate. It was locked. After a quick look around she put her foot on the lower bar of the gate and climbed over the police signs. The path to the towers looked more welcoming than the last time she was there. She could see the gaunt structures clearly. One was built on pillars placed in a circle with the grey stone above containing the water vessel on top. By its side, a much earlier structure of red brick rose from the ground, not unlike the ramparts of a castle.

The nearer she got to them; it was evident that neither structure was in use as a water tower. A blackened oak door with iron hinges was the only entrance to the earlier red brick structure and the door hung slightly open. Something moved in the grass beside it and Lisa froze. Surrounding the towers, the woods looked dark and menacing. She wondered what animal may have been taking refuge, and then calming down, she reminded herself that this was after all Cheshire and the only wild life around were probably foxes, badgers; and hedgehogs; certainly not deer in these woods. Lyme Park maybe, but that was miles away.

The rustling stopped and a black cat appeared, walking slowly towards her mewing.

'My God.' She stopped, recognising it as Jenny Simkins' cat. What's more, it looked in reasonable condition as if it had been fed regularly. She bent over and held out her hand making those sounds that cat lovers do. It surveyed her with its green eyes and then slinked off into the woods.

Lisa straightened up and watched it disappear leaving her with a hunch that its owner would not be far off either, and was in half a mind to go and investigate further. But something else caught her eye. The blue and white tape across the gate to Ravens Nest had been broken and was fluttering in the breeze and the gate was wide open. It was not a good sign.

Lisa walked over and after hesitating for a few moments, walked through and followed the path to the back door, which was swinging open on its big hinges. Someone had either gone in or come out. She hadn't seen anyone and who else would use the lane?. No cars had come through the tower gates; there was a padlock on it after all, and nobody was in the garden.

A dark foreboding settled over Lisa, Jenny's cat, the open gate and the back door to the house open. It didn't look at all good. What if Jenny Simkins was involved and was now looking for Hugo.

Lisa stepped into the kitchen; her first intention was to use her mobile to call for backup, and then decided against it. She didn't want to meet with the super's wrath again just yet. She could be totally wrong and realized Hugo may have just gone for a walk, forgetting to close the door and gate behind him. Her instinct still told her it very unlikely that he would be so absentminded.

Lisa refrained from asking for backup. Instead she moved in the direction of the hall, telling herself she would come up with something if confronted.

Voices were coming from the lounge. She turned to retrace her steps, and then stopped. One of those voices sounded familiar and it wasn't Hugo's.

What was Ted doing there? She stopped. Was it him who had entered the house by the rear door? Who ever it was must have been in a hurry or . . . .

The volume of the voices grew louder; Lisa crept close to the door which was not quite closed and peeped around. Hugo was standing by the window, he looked bewildered and worried and Ted's back was towards her. Hugo had put up both hands, palms facing outwards in a gesture of telling his opponent to quieten down and back off; his voice unsteady and eyes flicking towards something that Ted held.

'Please, I don't understand, what is it you want from me. Please put down the gun. We can talk.'

Lisa froze; one part of her was ready to quietly retreat and use her mobile, while the other part saw Hugo's life in danger and might be lost by the waiting. Somehow she needed to get Ted off guard and hope Hugo would take a chance and get the gun. Her mind was in a turmoil of disbelief and shock.

Ted was now doing the talking; so full of venom and hatred she hardly could believe it came from the same person she had shared intimate moments with.

'I'll tell you a story Ravenscroft, although you must be aware of it, for it is all to do with your wealth and our poverty.'

Hugo looked confused and began to say something but was quickly cut off.

'Your lot benefitted from lies and murder and prospered at our expense. We had only the poor glebe land from the church; good farmers like us quickly became a charity cause.'

'What the dickens are you talking about man?' Some authoritarian manner had crept into Hugo's voice over-riding the tentative position he now found himself in.

The laugh that broke from Ted's mouth had all the markings of an unstable mind. Lisa's body was trembling; suddenly she felt out of her depth. This was a Ted she didn't know at all. His words were now coming quickly.

'I'm talking about our land, the Greenfield's land that the Ravenscroft's took by giving false evidence;' his voice now rising in exasperation.

Lisa leaned closer to the crack in the door.

'Your lot accused Beth Simkins of witchcraft, remember.' He waited for a response and then getting none, continued as if it was a relief to get the whole thing out. 'Beth Simkins was a Greenfield before she married. The Ravenscrofts drove the whole family out and we ended up with poor glebe land. You stole our land. We changed our name to Green and managed to rent the glebe land. Did you know that?'

Hugo was staring in amazement at his assailant. 'Good God man, that was centuries ago. What's it got to do with me?'

Ted's laugh was high pitched, his arm moved as if positioning his gun for use.

'You benefitted no less and all the dammed Ravenscrofts before you, whilst I watched my father and grandfather before him die from hard work, little hope, and always begging for more time to pay their dues to the church. The land's poor; always has been and the work was always for someone else's benefit.' The venom in his voice took on a different tone, controlling and calculating.

"When I was a lad your dad ordered me off the land that had once been ours and I remembered Beth Simkins's curse. It spoke to me in my dreams every night and I knew I was the chosen one to fulfill her last wishes.'

Hugo's voice was now quiet and resigned as if he knew not to antagonise the man before him.

'You killed my sister Kristen.' It was more of a flat statement than a question.

'Fair's fair, someone had to pay the piper.' Ted laughed a little hysterically and for a moment lowered his arm a fraction. Lisa saw her chance, hurling herself at Ted's back, and at the same time yelling at Hugo to get the gun.

Whatever Lisa had planned didn't happen that way and she found herself lying flat on the floor holding a painful wrist and staring down the barrel of a gun. Hugo was frozen to the spot; his face ashen.

Ted leered at Lisa. 'Not so clever my girl, are you?' He looked at her with contempt. 'It wasn't the bedroom antics I was after; just the pillow talk, and you couldn't stop telling me what was going on at police headquarters.'

Lisa felt like someone had taken all her dignity away and wished he'd just hurry up and end it all.

Chapter 32

The silence in the room was broken only by sound of rapid breathing. The ticking of the clock and the outside traffic noise had seemed to fade away.

Lisa stared at Ted in complete disbelief and realized she was facing a very dangerous and disturbed man. She racked her brains for any signs that she'd failed to see in their relationship but found none; only the hint of dominance, if thwarted, in any plans he had in mind. His face too had changed; the eyes piercing and cunning, the mouth now turned into a permanent snarl. None of her training had equipped her for this situation and she felt at a loss.

Her wrist throbbed; her body shook and the choking feeling was getting worse. She swallowed and found herself listening to her own hardly recognisable voice.

'How did you get Kristen to go to the shed?' She heard Hugo wince, and the laugh that came from Ted was high and shrill, as if he enjoyed their sorrow.

'Easy, the dumb woman was besotted by her husband and would do anything to hold onto him. I just told her I had evidence of Tilstone cooking the mill's books and she offered me money for my silence.' This time his laugh sent shivers down Lisa's spine as he added spitefully, 'silly bitch.'

Hugo made to step forward, but a quick movement of the gun stopped him short.

But Lisa couldn't just leave it there, even if this was the final episode of her short life, she had to know the answers to his obsession with the Ravenscroft family.

'But the professor and John, how do they fit into all this?'

Ted's attention turned to Lisa, and she had the feeling he regarded her as some insignificant wounded animal about to be put down; once he had shown her how clever he was.

'Ah, that clever professor. You could say he started it all, just like his ancestors did.' Ted knew he was about to impart something surprising and he waited to gain their full attention, but none came. He stiffened and his features contoured. 'Did you know his ancestry line came from Matthew Hopkins?'

The blank looks that followed served only to fuel his anger. 'He's the bloody witch hunter who burnt people.'

'Oh.' Lisa responded with a groan, now realising the historical implications of what Ted was getting into.

'Clever chap that professor; he had charts galore of all the Simkins and Greenfield lands, but his big mistake was wearing the toadstone.' Ted looked at them as if they should see his point and understand. 'I had to have it.' Then a dark frown crossed his face and he could hardly get a word out that made any sense.

'After seeing it on his hand, the prof had to go; so I dispatched him.' He laughed. 'I always keep a knife with me; a useful thing for a farmer to have.' He chuckled, and then his face became blank again, as if everything that followed was just routine.

'Took the ring and papers and left and that could have been that, if that silly bugger Tilstone hadn't seen me coming out of the room.'

'What was John doing there?' It was the first time Hugo had spoken, he appeared resigned that he was facing a mad man but still baffled by it all.

Again that nasty laugh broke out.

'It was John Tilstone who opened the letter that the professor wrote to you. You and your sister didn't know what snake you had within your four walls.'

'So after seeing you come out of the room and hearing about the professor's death, he tried to blackmail you too.' Lisa's mind was racing as it clicked all these pieces together. Ted looked at her admiringly.

'Didn't work out though. I was too clever for him; not only shot him but threw the bugger out of the window.'

'Like garbage.' muttered Lisa, recalling the words of the police profiler, but she really needed to hear it from the killer. She'd got her answer.

'Not really, the window just happened to be open.'

'You're bloody mad.' spat out Lisa, voicing the only conclusion she could come to.

The gun now aimed at her heart and the finger on the trigger tightened a fraction.

That moment however was held suspended, as a voice came from the doorway and another figure appeared.

Jenny Simkins came forward. The very sight of her was disturbing, stirring up images from ancient books on witchcraft and witches. Small and frail, her hair hung around her face, dirty and uncombed. She wore a long black skirt; stained and partly torn in holes. A black sweater held bits of foliage and pollen; her skin white and the pale blue iris of her eyes pinpointing the small black spots of her pupils.

She carried a staff, old and knarled; her dirty fingers gripping the top of it like a vice.

Ted stepped back in horror, his eyes darting from one person to another, not knowing which one was the more dangerous.

'Enough.' Jenny lifted the staff pointing it at Ted. 'This has to end here and now.' The frail Jenny was gone and in its place; the nightmare of many a child.

Something moved, and a cat's head appeared, stroking her legs as it passed, then sat; its eyes glinting as it watched the drama unfolding.

All at once Ted laughed, the tone was high and shrill. 'Christ Jenny, I thought you were Beth come back to life.'

Jenny didn't move, but just surveyed the inmates of the room. 'It's over Ted.' she said simply.

Ted's voice changed into a childlike whining.

'Come on Jenny; we have the same blood line. Beth Simkins was a Greenfield before she married.'

Lisa made a slight noise and he turned to her mockingly. 'Learning a lot are you?'

Lisa's thoughts were on the conversation she'd had with the old man at the farm. She now realised he had mentioned Greenfield but she thought he'd said green fields at that time.'

Ted was now talking in a childlike manner.

'Jenny love, I could bring our family's curse to fruition at this very moment and with that ring you are wearing, we could disappear and buy new lands: A great new start for our family and the Ravenscroft family gone forever.' His vision so clear, he failed to see the contempt in her eyes.

Hugo broke in with a little laugh.' You are wrong there, I am not the last.'

Everyone looked to Hugo, and to everyone's surprise he was smiling. 'I have a son.'

The stunned look on Ted's face told Lisa that all of hell's fire was about to break out.

The blood rushed to Ted's face; his eyes maniacal, as he turned to face Jenny.

She nodded. 'Peter is Hugo's son,' she confirmed with a slight secretive smile and began pulling off her ring. Ted watched her, his eyes narrowing, not sure now which way to go.

Suddenly the ring came off her finger and she flung it on the floor.

Everything else then happened quickly, Ted stepped forward, Lisa flung her foot out and Ted tripped and started to fall. A single shot was fired as Hugo leapt on the falling man.

When Lisa came too, she was being lifted into an ambulance. She caught sight of Jiten talking to the paramedic. He turned, gave her the thumbs up sign and disappeared. Something was stuck into her arm. It was a tube attached to a plastic bag. A face smiled down at her.

'You will be fine, the bullet went right through your leg, we need to get you fixed up at the hospital, so relax and let us take charge now.'

They must have given her something for she slipped back into oblivion and didn't awake again until she was being pushed through the hospital doors.

Four hours later after the discomfort of the X-ray and examination tables, she sat up in bed, with her wrist plastered and elevated, and her leg bandaged on a pillow with a cage over it. A nurse hovered over her, about to connect her to a machine to record her vital signs

Suddenly she felt very thirsty and motioned her need. A brown hand handed her a glass of water, and Jiten's face followed as he bent over her.

'Silly bugger,' he said reprimanding her, before grinning at her; the relief in his eyes at her safety very evident.

'Case closed.' She uttered and managed to smile a little. Jiten looked uncomfortable wondering which way to play the conversation.

'Ted Green's been charged on all counts of murder and is undergoing a psychiatric examination at this moment.'

The patient closed her eyes for a second, as if trying to come to terms with the real Ted. 'Mad as a hatter, right?'

Jiten looked sympathetic and nodded. She turned her head away and gazed at the pattern on the screen surrounding her bed. Jiten tried to change her line of thought and all that had transpired.

'They're fixing up a private room for you, own TV and all.'

'Don't sound so envious Jiten, I'm not on vacation.'

Jiten looked at her sadly. Her suspension from the force could be called a vacation he supposed, but he wasn't going to be the one to tell her.

A familiar voice and face followed the huge bunch of flowers being thrust around the screen.

'You will do as you are told young lady, and when you are fit to come home I'll suffer no nonsense.'

Rita had turned into that once-efficient nurse again overnight, and Lisa knew there would be no arguing with her.

'Where's Ernest?' she asked trying to sit up a little.

'He's at the police station,' came the reply.

'Are Hugo and Jenny alright?'

Rita nodded. 'They're being checked over.' She gave a small laugh. 'Must say Jenny looks better after her bath and a good meal.'

'But where the hell was Jenny for all those weeks after her release?' enquired the patient.

'Remember the water towers behind the Ravencroft house.' Lisa nodded waiting for Jiten to continue, but all he did was to get up, as a nurse was signalling time to go.

Rita too was moving; she checked her watch, saying she had to pick up Ernest. Lisa stared after them, and sleep overcame her as the medications tripped in and she dozed off.

Chapter 33

It was Lisa's first time out to socialize, although few people would call it that when the people she was with, remained the same one's she'd been with for the past three weeks, namely her regular visitors. The difference was that the place of assembly had changed. Instead of entertaining her guests from her couch in number 7, she had allowed her friends to wheelchair her into the Horseshoe.

Ignoring the stares and whispers, Lisa tried to look in control of herself as Ernest manoeuvred her chair to a reserved table by the window. God, it was so good to be out and among people again, thought Lisa and smiled happily at Ernest as he asked whether she was ok. Her response lifted his spirits as she replied.

'Great, really great, and what would make the icing on the cake would be a pint of draught bitter.'

He raised his eyebrows slightly giving her a little salute and left her to the administrations of his wife.

'Comfy?' asked Rita, pulling up a chair.

Lisa smiled a grateful smile that she'd perfected over the last few weeks, although her inner self shamefully was saying something else, being quite fed up with being treated like an invalid. However it was great to be out of her house.

'Ah Jiten,' Lisa's face lit up as she welcomed the newcomer to the table, and to her surprise spotted Dr. Potts also manoeuvring himself between the tables and making his way to over to theirs.

She looked at them both with a certain amount of pleasure and nodded whilst raising her glass that Ernest had slipped in front of her. Within a short period all were seated and looking at her for confirmation on her progress.

'I'm doing just fine.' she said, glancing at Jiten to warn him off tapping her leg.

She hated the silly smiles that tried to cover up the real issue. Dam it all, they all knew she'd been suspended pending further investigations.

However the subject was not raised and a little part of her was grateful. She didn't want to get tearful in the Horseshoe of all places; bad enough the curious looks that came her way.

'So what's new?' the remark sounded childish and she regretted it right away. These were her friends and were concerned about her.

Jiten was the first to speak.

'Ted Green's been charged, but having trouble finding a lawyer. Who wants to defend a psychopath?' he stopped short, his brown face looking bewildered. 'What made him kill all those people? Nobody has explained anything to me as yet; only that they are sure they have the right person this time.'

He blushed at Lisa's glare.

It was Ernest that began clearing the air, and looked towards the doctor; who nodded for him to carry on.

'I think I can answer your question Jiten, daft as it may seem.' Ernest took a long drink before moving forward in his chair and pushing his glass out of the way.

'It all began four hundred years ago, right here on our doorstep.' He paused; waiting for their undivided attention before continuing.

'There were three families that owned land down where mill is now.' Ernest bent his elbow holding up three fingers then folding each one as they were named; 'Simkins, Greenfield and Ravencroft.'

Lisa cut in,

'In an earlier conversation with an old farm hand at Ted's farm, I hadn't realised he was referring to Ted's family by name. I just thought he meant the green fields around the farm.' Everyone stared at her. She blushed and coughed.

Ernest continued. 'The river however only ran through the Simkins land; making the soil fertile and the family very wealthy, leaving the Greenfield and Ravencroft families with generally dry and unproductive land. It only took a couple of years of drought to make them quite desperate. However the Greenfield family had a daughter who must have had many charms, as the owner of the Simkins land married her. The Ravencroft family were now finding themselves out in left field, so to speak.' Ernest awaited a comment. None came.

'Now we have to go back to the mood of the country in the 1600s.

When James 1 came to the throne he followed the practice of witch-trials that were popular in France and Germany, and Scotland had already been persecuting witches for some time.

Anyway James really got into it, and wrote a book on demonology, and he appointed a witch hunter; a fellow called Matthew Hopkins, who was given the grand title of 'Witchfinder General.'

Ernest took a long drink from his glass, and although the room bussed with chatter, their table seemed like a quiet oasis as they waited for him to continue.

'From what I read, it seemed that for a couple of centuries there were nearly fifty thousand folks that had been accused, tortured and killed on the Continent. As I said, King James was drawn in, being fascinated with the occult.'

For a moment there was total silence before he dropped another one of his surprises.

'One of the Witch-Finder General's descendants was our Professor Reece.'

'Bloody hell,' someone added, but the comment was hardly noticed as Ernest continued.

'Hopkins was a fanatical Puritan and who, even in those days would have been classified as a sadist. Trained as a lawyer, but failing in his chosen profession.'

Lisa now seemed to come out of a glazed state after listening to a history lesson and wanted to get on with where all this was leading.

'Oh, get on with it; we are now in the twenty-first century.' Jiten coughed over his drink, as Ernest continued with his diatribe on English history without being fazed by her remarks.

'The Ravenscroft family made an accusation against Beth Simkins, seizing on the fact that her husband had died suddenly from unknown causes. Their own crops had again failed and probably a few of their animals had died too. Anyway folks around were frightened and were more than glad to see the Witchfinder General come to save them from the devils spawn. There was probably a deal between the two parties and both profited. It was most likely that the Ravencroft family got both the Simkins and the Greenfield lands.' 'Bloody hell!' Everyone turned to look at Lisa in amazement and whose face had now flushed a bright red.

Ernest sat back; his job completed and he nodded to Dr Potts to take up the story.

'Beth's old nurse took Beth's child and disappeared. Beth was burnt at the stake in Chester and the Greenfield family were pushed off their land. The Ravenscroft family took all; and no doubt the Witchfinder General lined his pockets too. He died very rich.'

'So that's why the professor came to town then, to learn more about his ancestor,' piped up Jiten.

'Yes, that's where his interest lay. He even wore a ring from that period.'

'A toadstone,' someone uttered. 'A toadstone ring?'

'Yes.' Ernest answered. 'Go on Potts.'

The doctor took a breath. 'Now we come to yet another story. When the old nurse left, she took with her a casket that belonged to the Simkins family. Alone with the young Simkins child, the old nurse managed to bring him up. However, because of his mother's violent and untimely death as a witch, he forsook the Simkins name and took on his foster mother's name.'

He stopped, took a breath, before adding. 'That name was Potts.' It took a while before the realization of his words to sink in.

He grew up, married, and had two sons. However the two sons chose who they wanted to be. One kept the name Potts and got on with his life, the other reverted back to the Simkins name and returned to their original land as a farm labourer. Jenny is the last of them, not forgetting Peter of course.'

'So you are related?' exclaimed Lisa,

'I'm afraid so,' the doctor smiled a little sadly.

Dr. Potts lifted his arm to the waiter indicating another round of drinks. All accepting; they waited for their glasses to be filled, then with renewed anticipation for the continuing saga to unfold.

Lisa at this point however was getting a little confused and her leg and back ached. 'I'm only interested in the homicides, all this talk of witches and name changing doesn't alter the fact a number of people have been murdered.' She stopped short; blushing a little before finding her voice again.

'So Ted was the last of the Greenfield family, and they had to rent glebe land that proved to fail as farmland. I know he's mad and blamed the Ravenscrofts; trying to kill the bloody lot of them. But now you are all talking of hidden boxes, the Potts family and bloody rings. I just don't get it.' Lisa sank back and rolled her eyes.

Rita shook her head and picked her drink up. 'It wasn't just about revenge Lisa, Ted wanted Jenny's ring.'

There was a feeling the people around the table had moved forward and at this moment were almost sitting in a huddle around the table as Rita was about to continue.

But Ernest broke in. 'Remember the Greenfield family were Beth Simkins' family too, she probably told her parents about the Simkins' diamond. It was flawless and extremely valuable and when things started to happen when Ralph died, Beth had her toadstone ring hollowed out and the diamond placed behind it. It was kept in a small casket with other documents and given to Martha Potts.'

'Ernest and I talked to an expert on the toadstones and knew Jenny's ring wasn't quite like the rest. That's why Ernest could distinguish it. It was bigger in shape and the colours slightly different.'

'So it was the ring that Ted was after. First to rid himself of the Ravenscrofts, get the toadstone ring with the diamond hidden in it from Jenny and live the rest of his life in luxury.'

'It must have been a shock to him when he found out Peter had Ravenscroft blood in him.' Jiten gave a small chuckle and Potts interrupted, with a small smirk of satisfaction on his face.

'Peter is not a Ravenscroft.'

'Not Hugo's?' Rita exclaimed.

'Oh yes, Peter is Hugo's child alright but not a Ravencroft. Hugo's real father is unknown, although Sara Simkins, the midwife who delivered Hugo probably knew all about it at the time by the colour of Hugo's blonde hair; and so would Jenny.'

Ernest is just loving this, thought Lisa; as she looked for the smirk on his face.

'The doctor and I found the casket behind the dresser at the cottage, where a cavity had been made in the stone wall. Peter had told Dr. Potts, he had seen his mother with the casket and ring at sometime or other, and had watched her putting it back into the wall cavity behind the dresser. Anyway we looked in it and found a few other interesting things. Apart from the ancient documents on land ownership and a lock of blonde hair twisted around a medieval cross, there was also a letter to Sara Simkins, the midwife to the Ravenscroft's, identifying Hugo's real father.

'Does Ted know this?' asked Lisa.

'Yes Jenny told him afterwards, and also that the diamond had vanished generations ago.'

Dr. Potts slumped back in his chair, and an odd smile crossed his face.

'I wonder_____?' he said it more to himself than anyone else. He looked back at them all around the table.

'There was an ancestor of mine in the eighteenth hundreds who went to Australia. He had no skills and little education, but seemed to have made it big out there; a sudden fortune by all accounts.'

He clapped his hands; 'I think the drinks are again on me.'

The End.

5101408R00119

Printed in Great Britain
by Amazon.co.uk, Ltd.,
Marston Gate.